Generation Ship

Adam Carpenter

First Edition
Published by Breaking Rules Publishing Europe, 2021.
This is a work of fiction. Similarities to real people, places, or events are entirely coincidental.
Generation Ship
978-91-986840-6-3
Copyright © 2021 Adam Carpenter.
Written by Adam Carpenter

A Note on Names

In the human sphere in the early 27th Century, it was the general custom, with some exceptions, for legal surnames to be formed in the style that had been used in Portugal and Brazil on Terra in the 21st Century (also known as the "Crisis Century"), with each person having two surnames. Generally - but not always - the first comes from their mother and the second from their father. However, only the latter would be used in most day-to-day contexts. Legal surnames did not change on marriage unless the person wished for this to occur.

Warrant Officer Sunita Kumar's full name is Sunita Kamala Anwar Kumar. However, she would not use that in full outside of an official document. For all 'everyday' purposes, she is known as Sunita Kumar. While of mostly Tamil heritage, her parents used a different spelling to the Tamil "Sunitha" to honour a great-grandmother.

Furthermore, the tradition in Poland, Russia, and that region of different surname endings for men and women fell out of use in the 23rd Century.

Prologue

Vault Nineteen was where stuff went to stay buried.

Max Govan, Branch Manager of the Lagos Branch of Swiss Bank Inc. was the only man on Terra with the access card to it. Sitting inside this underground bunker below his bank sat a whole string of items that had been placed there, sometimes centuries before, in the safety deposit boxes and dedicated vault rooms.

The boxes and vaults were rented for decades at a time. The boxes could only be opened via someone providing a set key phrase, when the accounts expired, after a court order or if they really, really started to smell.

The paper ledger in front of him right now was, in fact, the fourth copy; it had been rewritten by hand as each previous example started to fall apart. He had added four entries himself in the ten years since he became manager here. Not that he knew what the contents of the boxes were of course – Swiss Bank were known for their discretion.

Although he often wondered. Especially 'Box 28', first opened in 2100, 519 years ago, by the now defunct West African Union, shortly after the destruction of Abuja by nuclear fire in an attack that had turned the western suburbs of Lagos into a charnel house.

The current lease ran up to 2700, by which point he would be long dead.

It was a vault room, the biggest they had, and the pass phrase was distinctly ominous.

It was 'Berchtesgaden is rebuilt'.

Chapter 1

Helvetios, also known as 51 Pegasi, was very much off the beaten track. Forty-eight light years from Sol, it held the dubious distinction of being the nearest habited system to Sol that was not accorded the status of a full state in the Terran Union – due to insufficient population. Instead, it was just a colony, run by an appointed Board of Commissioners.

The half a million inhabitants mostly worked in the many mines spread out across the system, as independent prospectors, or in other associated industries. The ore was placed into transport pods, which were docked onto the array of cargo ships that could be found in orbit at any one time, before being shipped to refineries in other systems, with those ships bringing back the food needed for the workers.

Like the Fast Transport Ship *Tulyar*, a medium general-purpose freighter of the Star Worker class, built forty years earlier. Its 240-metre length, not anywhere near some of the behemoths out there that could easily exceed a kilometre, meant that it was far too large to land and take off on a planet.

In any event, you know when you were looking at a Star Worker.

A boxy front compartment contained the living space for the crew and was topped with a double-barrelled cannon firing unguided shells that had to be 'manually' loaded. This was good for self-defence against another civilian ship, but not a military vessel.

Six powerful engines were contained in a similarly boxy aft section along with a fission reactor; the drives giving the ship an impressive turn of acceleration and hyper speed that had saved the lives of those on board more than once. It was fast for a cargo hauler even now.

Between this sat a bulging cargo area, itself not pressurised except for a small corridor area liking the front and back. The bay, accessible by large doors currently open to reveal their contents, contained four docking arms where standard container modules could be attached, larger bulk units or even cargo lighters.

In terms of colouring, the ship itself was painted greyish blue, with yellow visibility panels at the front and rear. This was a holdover from a previous owner that no-one had ever bothered to change. Even the current owners had merely stuck their flag on the side.

All of this made *Tulyar* a rather distinctive and memorable vessel, in a 'classic car' sense. They generally got interest from at least one enthusiast at the bigger stations.

And there had been one such enthusiast in the New London Merchant Marine Corporation, also known as the New London Merchant Navy. Four months previously, it had been unloading its cargo of freezers on the planet when Customs had found some medicine in the shipment that was not on the manifest.

The whole cargo had been seized and to cover the shortfall in their income as a result, the crew of the then Independent Transport Ship *Tulyar* had decided to engage in a risky prison break operation on a jungle planet.

They had rescued three prisoners... who on arriving in New London all succumbed to a virus – a virus injected into their system by the regime that had imprisoned them. Fortunately for everyone else concerned, Kongzhi-C was deliberately made not to be contagious.

Now facing smuggling and biosecurity charges, the captain of *Tulyar* agreed to surrender his ship to New London in exchange for not being personally prosecuted. Given the choice between working for a corporation and unemployment, some of the crew decided to stay on, now working for the New London Merchant Navy.

None of them could have known the consequences of their decision.

For what was about to unfold would be the biggest event of the lives of the twenty-two humans on board *Tulyar* – and possibly the last.

For the contents of Box 28 were about to be unveiled...

****

Director James Shepherd of the Helvetios Deep Space Monitoring Network was just finishing his vat grown pork wrap in his small but well-furnished office when his desk telephone rang. He swallowed his current mouthful and pressed the speaker phone button.

"What is it, Tran, and why can't it wait until after lunch?" he groaned with the weary resignation of someone who often had his lunch interrupted.

"We've just picked up a new contact entering the system by sub-light," Shift Leader Milos Tran replied, his voice sounding overly excited. "Well, I say just picked up. Zug Station picked it up on their sensors a day ago and sent over one of their ships to look closer."

The Deep Space Monitoring Networks, with their array of telescopes, radar sites and light scout craft, monitored the space in and around their systems for things that could pose a danger. This far into Terran Union space, it was nearly always errant space rocks.

"Slow down, Milos. Sub-light? So fast, but not a hyper exit?"

The Shift Leader took a breath and did so as Shepherd took a sip of his apple juice.

"The scout ship just jumped into orbit around this planet and sent its report, so the latest data is two hours old at present. Speed 0.1c according to the blue shift. I'll send you through the detection details. It's a biggie. Edward's drafting the message for the BeaconGram message to Sol as I speak."

If Edward was sending a message to Sol via the hyperspace Beacon Network, the fastest way to relay messages between star systems (at a text-only rate of transmission), then this detection was of great significance indeed.

Shepherd moved to look at the screen as the new contact data appeared on it. He lowered his cup to view it as Tran continued.

"530 AU out and *de-accelerating* at 9 metres per second squared, which is just less than 1G."

Shepherd knew that of course, but let Tran carry on.

"That is not normal behaviour for an extra-solar asteroid. And a freighter will not exit hyper at that distance unless it is in *serious* trouble," Tran observed.

"Yes, that's not normal behaviour," Shepherd remarked. Asteroids *accelerated* as they approached a star, they did not slow down.

"No standard distress signals either. Just a series of Morse pulses, which we've managed to decode. 1799 binary digits, with some text included at the end."

Tran is barely containing his enthusiasm at this, Shepherd thought to himself.

Shepherd scrolled down. He was looking at a picture with a whole string of complex coded elements that only an intelligent life form would understand. A human figure, DNA, a depiction of the Sol system and its eight planets, plus various other elements. His mouth dropped open.

Wow, it's an Arecibo beacon. He's justified in his reaction to this. It's a career maker.

The Arecibo beacon was a digital message based, with some minor changes, on the first major message sent out to the cosmos from Terra back in the 20th century. With elements of it used in an array of Terran Union iconography, including the flag of the Sol System Republic, even a child could recognise it.

"Way to bury the lead, Tran! That means... that means... it's a Generation Ship from Sol. Name of *Rosa Parks*. How often is this transmitting?"

Shepherd opened his word processor programme to type some notes.

"On repeat sir," Tran responded. "Every ten minutes. The signal is weak at the moment, of course. It is five light days out, but it won't be long before ships in-system start picking up the transmission."

"You are right, it is a biggie... We've not found one of those for decades..."

"Once they figure out it's an Arecibo beacon, this will be *galaxy*-wide news... In any event, we will need to send a request for cross checking the database of the human colony ships back on Terra, sir. The records here don't seem to have the name *Rosa Parks* on them. That will take about six hours to come back; two hours each way with the latest encryption standard. At least. Depends on the traffic on the Beacon Network."

The Colonial Office in Sol would have the central data on this ship. This *was* technically their ship, even it had not been seen for four or five centuries and had been almost certainly been commissioned for a private company.

Probably from one of the North American countries judging by the name, he thought.

Director Shepherd took another mouthful of his wrap.

There's a protocol here, we need to follow it.

He opened another window on his terminal and searched through the procedure manuals, quickly finding the one that covered this situation.

Inform Sol, check. Get the ship secured. Secure a quarantine and debriefing facility on the surface. Secure suitable medical supplies...

"Get that message sent," he said. "In the meantime, we need to get this vessel secured before the cat gets out of the proverbial bag and we get a carnival of onlookers. What's the closest fast ship in this system now?"

"I'll contact Traffic and Station Control and get back to you," Tran said. "Be back in ten minutes."

"Got it."

Director Shepherd waited for eight minutes, during which time he finished his lunch. His mind ran all over the exciting possibilities of what they could find on that ship. Even if it was full of corpses, the archaeological significance was huge.

As he was polishing off his apple juice, Tran called back.

"You've spoken to TSCA?" Shepherd asked, referring to the Traffic and Station Control Agency that handled civilian space traffic and station operations.

"Yes, I have. The fastest ship would be the New London-flagged freighter *Tulyar*, it appears. Speed factor one hundred. The System Defence Destroyer is on the other side of our star... but it's got a faulty hyperdrive. We have a *Personality* survey ship, but that can only do ninety and would need back-up in any event. TSCA are going to call for a large hospital ship too. Our one is over in Steph 2065, helping that mining ship that got into difficulty."

"Yes, don't know what they were doing there. So, we're going cap in hand to the farmers of New London for this. Well, I suppose they could do with the money." Shepherd remarked.

"Not my fault this is a backwater system. Although I'm wondering why the GenShip came here," Tran mused.

"The surveyors made an error in the temperature calculations when they first mapped this place from afar."

"Not what I was saying. This is *really* far from home."

****

Warrant Officer Sunita Kumar, Security and Safety Officer of *Tulyar*, was in the ship's weapon room, counting ammunition - or rather getting Grant Robinson, their new apprentice, to count it for her. Rank had its privileges and deferring boring tasks to the new guy was one of them.

Sunita Kumar was a brown skinned human being aged twenty-four who would be described as South Asian but had never been within ten parsecs of the subcontinent. She had a five-centimetre growth of black hair currently under a wig, a big mouth, and a pointy chin. She was short and slightly chubby due to some baby fat she had not managed to shift, which was a slight irritant, but not something she lost sleep over.

She was already losing plenty of it because of her baby daughter Kimberley anyway.

"642 rounds of 10mm full metal jacket rifle ammunition," Grant said.

Sunita wrote that number on the digital pad in front of her and watched as the handwriting was converted into printed form.

"Got it," she said. "Put those back and we'll deal with the pistol ammunition next..."

She turned her head quickly and her wig did not keep up.

"Ma'am," Grant said.

"I know," Sunita sighed and pulled it off, then removed the wig cap to reveal her natural hair.

Grant got up and started to put the boxes of ammunition back into the cupboard.

"I saw an interesting report from New London in *Larynx*."

Sunita scratched an itch on her leg.

"That's a horrendous name for a magazine, but I've heard good things about their writing," she responded.

"Apparently some woman escaped from a military prison in Bangla with one of her warders and is claiming that she was present when one of their ships destroyed a prison colony with a nuclear weapon four months ago," Grant reported.

"Well, they did," Sunita snarled. "That's why I've got this stupid thing."

Sunita held up the wig.

"Yes, you said. The radiation made your hair fall out."

"Then some other stuff happened that I'm not legally allowed to talk about. Then the New London Merchant Navy got this ship and me. Hurry up, will you?"

She reached inside her shirt pocket to pull out some bubble gum.

"How long have we got orbiting this dump of a planet?"

"Probably another day. The frozen food is off loaded, now we're waiting for them to transfer the ores up."

"Then off to Chalawan," she said, then popped a fresh piece of gum into her mouth.

"Indeed. Off to Chalawan. Another step on the long and winding road to Sol."

"Yes, I'm looking forward to going there."

"So am I, but that's probably another month away at least. Let's focus on the task at hand."

The conversation ended there and there was silence for about two minutes as Grant moved the ammunition around. Then the internal intercom rang.

Sunita walked over to it and picked up the receiver.

"Kumar, it's the Captain," came the voice of Vanessa Widomski, Captain of *Tulyar.* "You are not going to believe what I have just been told." Vanessa was sounding pretty 'normal', which considering that she normally had a general ice queen demeanour, meant this was big.

"Let me guess, they finally have a perfume you like?" Sunita asked, blowing a bubble.

"I can only hope," Vanessa remarked wistfully. "No, Deep Space Monitoring have – and it's four months after April Fool's Day – apparently found a GenShip."

Sunita took a second to process that. Then another three. She let the bubble deflate, then spat the gum out into the nearby bin.

"A GenShip? An honest Earth colony ship, out here? Holy..." she began to exclaim.

There was a clatter as Grant dropped a box of bullets in shock. Sunita put her tablet down.

"There are apparently twenty unaccounted for. We're only forty-eight light years from Sol, so finding one from five centuries back is possible. They could only really do 0.1c."

Sunita did some quick mental arithmetic.

"Which means we'd be looking at something from the second generation of those vessels, circa 2119."

"The first mass departure of humanity from Sol, yes."

"The invention of hyper technology in the late 22nd century resulted in most of the ships still out in deep space being found by later generations and their passengers picked up... so there aren't exactly many left to find."

We then had to orientate the 'icicles' to the changes in the galaxy while they were asleep. I remember watched a documentary featuring one of those people a few years back, Sunita thought.

"That's correct, Mrs Kumar," Vanessa audibly beamed. "You know your stuff."

"That's Fourth Year History, everyone knows that. Do we know which one?" Sunita asked.

"Apparently goes under the name *Rosa Parks* but it's not in the encyclopaedia system as one of them. They're sending a secure message via Beacon to Sol to check their records. Not all the ships were properly recorded. I know some of the Spacee ships weren't."

Sunita mentally nodded, then replied. Spacees (or Spacers if you were being formal) were members of a nomadic group that formed a major part of the interstellar travelling community. While they had their roots from various nomadic or itinerant peoples on pre-Space Terra, there were Spacees from all human ethnic groups. Indeed, an increasingly number of humans did not think themselves of any ethnicity except simply as a human.

Six of the crew of *Tulyar* were Spacees including Sunita, Daniel, Kimberley (technically not a crew member of course), and Vanessa. A far cry from the fifteen who had been present when this was an independent trading vessel. They tended to be reluctant to work for governments and even more so for military forces.

Although "we don't work for governments" is a very flexible term. New London Merchant Navy is really just a nationalised company and actually a decent employer.

"I can trace my ancestry back to a couple who fell in love on GS *Wisconsin*," Sunita replied. "That ship wasn't registered. Caused a bit of a kerfuffle when it reached its destination at the same time as another lot of colonists..."

Vanessa interrupted her, now more serious.

"System government want this vessel secured and out the way before a circus starts. We're the fastest ship in the system, so we're tasked with making first contact – also a civilian ship will be less scary. We're picking up a military science vessel that will be along for the ride, and there's a medical ship coming in a couple of days.

"At any rate, I am recalling the entire crew from the surface, ready to go in four hours. The containers are going to be detached and the ore transport is going to another vessel, but we'll still get paid our fee.

"Full briefing in three hours. Read up on the health & safety aspects. As head of safety, I want you on the party. I also want you to select its members, subject to my approval."

"Why me?" Sunita asked, with an air of curiosity and surprise.

"Because you're the best I have on the safety front. You'll pick who is right for the job without playing favourites... and you need a challenge. This will look great for your commission application."

"Who says I want a commission?"

"You did, last Saturday. After three shots of Stolichnaya. *In vodka veritas.* Now get on with your task, Mrs Kumar."

****

Sunita Kumar returned to her room to start planning what she was going to say in her part of the briefing. She was not sure of the safety requirements for such an operation as this. No-one had picked up a colony ship for nearly thirty years and while there was a general procedure, it was deep in the manuals somewhere. She would have to search through the Guild database stored on *Tulyar* on what to do.

As she opened the door, she came face to face with a muscular red-haired man dressed only in boxer shorts, holding a pair of handcuffs and a can of whipped cream.

I forgot I had plans, Sunita mused.

She swore under her breath. The latest episode of their new sex game was going to have to wait,

But he looks so eager and hot... Oh, let's just do it.

She closed the door, lay on the bed, removed her wig, and started to unbutton her shirt as Daniel O'Hanlon flipped open the can.

"I've got some urgent work to do, but I'm happy to do it nearly naked and with whipped cream in my hair..."

"So, question one," came the voice of her husband.

****

Captain Vanessa Widomski was a Slavic woman in her early forties with curly black hair that stopped just above her shoulders and a figure that had in the past attracted attention from modelling agencies. She had rejected their offers for the more dangerous - but more financially secure - environment of interstellar travel.

She was currently stood at ease on the bridge of her vessel, looking out of the window at the hot mining planet of Basel.

Unlike her home planet of New London, you could not really grow much more than cacti at the poles here. Only the lights of landing bays indicated where the under-surface habitation was located.

"I've got a departure window from the station," David Forgan, the ship's chief pilot said, swinging his chair around to face her. "We're cleared to go at 1800 hours local time with a thirty-minute slot."

"Thank you, Mr Forgan," Vanessa said. "Ms Qarpik, you have that information, so please set a course to our next destination."

As boatswain Lyta Qarpik, currently sitting in the navigator's seat, started to run a navigation plot, Vanessa Widomski walked towards her Captain's chair.

The artists of the early Space Age had generally conceived their spaceship interiors as cool and clinical places with grey or white walls, filled with futuristic computer banks and seats filled with strapping people not actually strapped in.

Tulyar had grey walls, but the whole area was far more lived in than those television shows, with various posters, guides and labels stuck all over the place in a way that would give a feng shui practitioner vivid nightmares. Nine consoles were dotted around, most of which could have their function changed by swapping the peripherals around.

Vanessa moved into her seat. This was a much more complex affair than the seats of lore with a four-point harness and box containing an emergency oxygen system that also served as a good place to rest a can of energy drink.

She pulled down one of the two monitors that were in their raised position and pressed the power button to turn the screen on. White text appeared against a black background.

FTS TULYAR NAVIGATION INFORMATION

CURRENT LOCATION: DOCKED TO 51
PEGASI STATION, BASEL, HELVETIOS
     DESTINATION: ZUG STATION, HELVETIOS
DISTANCE TO DESTINATION: 101 AU
TRAVEL TIME IN CONVENTIONAL SPACE:
21 HOURS, 16 MINUTES (ESTIMATED)

"That's far too long a trip by sub light, Lyta, you should have known that. Please check on the charts where the hyper limit is," Vanessa signed.

"Sorry, ma'am," Lyta said and moved to her keyboard to make some changes.

Vanessa moved to switch on the holographic display table and lower the screen above it that was used for presentations. A 3D map of the Helvetios system appeared and she zoomed out to show the projected locations of both Zug Station and Rosa Parks.

"New course plotted, Captain. Journey time of five hours ten minutes."

The course appeared on the display, with drive settings, hyper entry and hyper exit points marked.

"Much better," Vanessa said.

****

Sunita and her spouse arrived on the bridge thirty seconds before Vanessa was due to start the briefing; the rest of the invitees were already present. They had their arms around each other, with a clear grin on their faces.

"Glad you could make it. Did you prepare the safety briefing?" Vanessa asked with a slight air of irritation.

This resulted in Sunita patting her pockets for a few seconds, swearing loudly and then disappear back into the corridor.

By the door to the Map Room, the ship's First Officer, Darius Marri, shrugged his shoulders.

"At it like rabbits," Vanessa said under her breath.

Sixteen crew members would be present at this briefing. Dr Wilmslow was looking after Kimberley Kumar O'Hanlon, who was now able to say about twenty words.

Sunita returned two minutes later, holding a handheld tablet in her pocket.

Vanessa took a deep breath, rang a hand bell, and brought everyone to attention.

"We've got ourselves a rather unique salvage mission. A Generation Ship," she said.

She smiled as waves of realisation appeared all over the faces of the present crew and loud discussion began.

I knew they would be excited, Vanessa observed. *And I've not even told them about the salvage fee.*

She rang the bell to obtain silence, tapped a few buttons and a holographic map of the Helvetios system appeared.

"Long-range tracking has discovered an Arecibo beacon about five hundred astronomical units out from the system primary. Those beacons, for those not familiar with their history, were fitted to all Generation Ships that would allow them to transmit information that they were from an intelligent species, a description of humanity and a crude image of the appearance of the ship. From the Morse transmission added at the end, we've identified the ship as a *Rosa Parks*, which doesn't appear to be in the main list of colony ships. A message is going to Sol asking for more information on that."

She paused, and a rough route appeared.

"We will be heading out to Zug Station in this system's Kuiper belt to meet with the Terran Union military survey ship *Emilia Plater*, skippered by a Commander Dirk. Then, we will with the GenShip and attempt to establish contact with the ship's complement. The system is asking for one of their hospital ships to come over, identity to be confirmed. That won't be for a day or two, so we won't take anyone off unless they're in a serious state."

"Now, no-one has interacted with one of these since 2590, which was when the *Lander Deutschland* was found near Castor, 490 years after leaving Sol. Sunita will give us some more information on the special safety considerations required when we board this vessel."

Sunita Kumar walked over to the table. As she stood, Vanessa saw something white next to a blue-button stud earring and leant forward.

"You got a bit of cream behind your right ear," Vanessa whispered.

At which point Sunita rolled her eyes and huffed.

"Yes, everyone, I made out with my husband! And it was a lot of fun. If you want tips on how to spice up your love life, send me a text message."

"Kumar, I'm fine with your kinky sex games, but we have a briefing to get on with," Vanessa told her.

"Sorry, ma'am."

"Carry on, Mrs Kumar."

****

Sunita then activated the screen, brought up her presentation and begun. Her presentation skills were not the best in the world, but they had considerably improved over time.

"Generation Ships are built very differently from modern ships. When you must travel for centuries with no access to spare parts, or extra fuel, you must be prepared for every eventuality... and deal with a lot of routine repair work. As a result, most of the ships had automated maintenance robots that swept the corridors, checking for faults and cracks in the infrastructure. The robots are designed to stop automatically when someone is present in the same corridor, but if they don't detect you, they may be travelling at a considerable speed. So, keep an eye on where you are going."

She started to take them through the presentation she had made earlier. As she talked, she noticed Grant Robinson and shuttle pilot Maria Penzance standing rather close to each other.

Well, well, Sunita thought, *A new romance on board... anyway, back to work.*

"We'll be taking in a team of ten and going in using indoor vacuum suits; the air might be a little stale. It may well be off in some sections. I'll make the decision closer to our actual arrival – I want to see who will be joining us from the survey ship."

Rebecca 'Becky' Carrington, the relatively new navigator and also Second Officer, slowly raised her red jacketed arm. A Caucasian brunette with long straight hair kept in a ponytail, she wore a loose-fitting floral dress along with her jacket and being only a few years older than Sunita, seemed to the Security Officer like the lead alto in a village choir. She did actually sing in the ship's band. Sometimes. She did not like the rude songs or the ones about sex.

"What about the overall temperature? Those suits are not really designed for excess of four hundred Kelvin – or under one hundred Kelvin either," Becky asked.

"We're not exactly going to be near a star," Sunita replied. "So, there's no real concern there. Also, we'll avoid any bits open to space. If the overall temperature is out of safety range, we'll switch to the harder suits. Since the ship is transmitting a signal, we're assuming other bits of power are still functioning."

She turned to a picture of the interior of a colony ship. It had been found in one of their electronic encyclopaedias and from a look that she noticed on Vanessa's face, Sunita suspected the Captain had figured that out.

"We're may well be dealing with zero gravity in large parts of the vessel, except for the habitation/cryo-sleep areas. It's less likely if the engines are running as the deacceleration will produce some 'gravity', but it might not be running the whole time.

"It is quite easy to get disoriented and to careen out of control. You have your air propulsion pistols, use them sparingly and carefully. Many of the corridors will be very narrow indeed, so you will basically have to crawl along them."

Sunita brought up an image of a cryogenic pod.

"We don't know what the condition of the people will be like inside. We've not found a pod that's been running for this long before. Judging by distance and speed, five hundred years is a realistic possibility. *Lander Deutschland* had been running for 420 years and three quarters of the pods had failed with the resulting deaths of those inside from sudden temperature change. They'd turned into mummies, basically. The rest had managed to activate their safety protocol, which is a more gradual defrost, but there were twenty people on board, half over fifty. Most of us are familiar with corpses from our lives already, but apparently you never forget your first mummy. I remembered that from the documentary I saw about *Lander Deutschland* a few years back."

Vanessa was about to harrumph, but David Forgan, spoke up at this point.

"Would everyone be asleep, or would there be people awake?"

"I think we have to be prepared for a small number of people to be up and about. However, we're going to be dealing with people who haven't had any contact with the rest of humanity for a few hundred years. The culture barrier is going to be large, the language barrier too. And our handheld translators aren't generally programmed with 22nd Century Terran languages... hopefully we can find a professional interpreter."

"Looks like we're going to need a lot of professionals for this job." David said.

"Yes, the plan is to get these people into some form of quarantine sharpish, although we need to wait for the hospital ship to do that. We don't know what viruses they might have... and we don't want to infect them with Vanessa's sense of humour."

"Ha hah," Vanessa replied.

****

As Sunita walked out the briefing room, her comm vibrated. She read the text message. It was from Becky Carrington, who wanted tips on how to spice up her love life with her new husband, Alexander, a Dougla man from New Guyana, who served as the ship's cargo chief.

Interesting, Sunita reflected. *She isn't such a 'traditional' woman after all. Changing your surname to your husband's is one of the signs of an Offred - but maybe I misjudged her.*

Then she switched over to the tasks the crew would need to engage in ready for their departure. She would need to make sure their spacesuits were functioning. She checked them on a weekly basis in any event, so there should not be any real problems, but a fault could be lethal.

An awesome sense of responsibility came over her. This is the sort of thing that a crew would only do once in a lifetime - if they were lucky.

Also, while she would not have to do massive parts of the 'debriefing' - that would be left to a fuller professional team once those arrived from Sol... but she would possibly be that ship's first contact with the rest of humanity for centuries.

I'd better make sure my wig is on straight then.

****

The large cargo doors of *Tulyar* swung open on each side and a small spaceship came out, bristling with antennae, from the port side. It moved away a short distance and then six large grey pods, each filled with ore, came out together, three from each side, a group of synchronised space swimmers.

Rebecca Carrington glanced at the situational display from her quarters as the impressive ballet continued with them moving apart from the ship; she had seen it before of course. Her husband was monitoring the operations of the robot control ship from the Cargo Control Centre, ready to intervene if things went wrong. The ore pods would then huddle around the control vessel, staying in formation until another ship could take them on board.

She herself had other tasks to do. The navigation tasks were relatively simple here provided you put in the correct inputs. Helvetios had a standard constellation of navigational satellites and you could get your position within the system from triangulating off them, factoring in the light speed lag. So, Layla could take care of that.

Rebecca herself was using her computer to write a quick orientation guide for the sleepers. There was a whole vast expanse of settled space to introduce them to after all. The five centuries since they had gone had seen humanity clamber out of the depths of despair, through adversity to the stars.

She reached a bit on religion and then thought of an apt biblical comparison. These were the innocent exiles from Israel, at last allowed back to Jerusalem. Or Abraham arriving in Canaan. What would they think of the galaxy they now found themselves in?

She looked up to the ceiling and prayed for God to guide the new arrivals in their time of utter confusion.

Then another inspiration came to her. With the money that she was going to get from this operation, she could afford to pay for her church's new organ. Then she would need to persuade the vicar not to put a great big plaque with her name on it...

It was going to be an interesting week.

****

On a ship five hundred astronomical units away from Helvetios, a blonde-haired woman put on her jacket and adjusted her lapel pin. It was a pin with a black eagle, wings spread, holding a wreath with a starred diagonal cross.

Chapter 2

Maria sat on the single bed, watching as her new boyfriend pored his way through the article on Spacepedia covering Generation Ships. They had subscriptions to six such encyclopaedias.

Grant Robinson was just over 18 years old, definitely cute, with short brown hair, some nice teeth, and a lovely nose. He was also well built from what she had seen so far. They had not gone all the way yet; neither felt quite ready for that.

She was a year older than him, with collar length black hair (a recent change in style) with a somewhat elven look and the distinctive accent of the Union of Irish Stars, hailing from the Antrim system. She had been in his place until three months ago, serving as an Apprentice on *Tulyar* and doing all the jobs that no-one else wanted to do.

Now she had transferred the mop and bucket to Grant Robinson.

"You know, I had a look at our bonus scheme on this ship," she said.

Grant stopped and turned to look at her.

"Really. What did it say?"

"If we engage in a major operation that brings great benefit to New London, be it economical or reputational, we're entitled to a bonus."

"Interesting…"

"And if we find something of great historical value – or a wanted fugitive, 50% of the reward fee is split among the crew. There's a ratio based on seniority that determines what each of us get."

"What do you think we'd get for a Generation Ship?"

"Take a look at the *Lander Deutschland* entry."

Grant found it and read through. It had been found by a mining ship named *Pierre Blanc*… which had netted eighteen million Terran credits.

"18 million… not a bad score… what would we get?"

"In my case…" Maria counted on her fingers as she did the maths, "forty-five thousand."

"For you, right? What about me?"

"Nada. You're an apprentice," she grinned. "But I might let you stay at the apartment I'll put a deposit on with it."

Grant got up.

"You're getting an apartment?"

"Looking to... getting a bit sick of the company section house. The superintendent is a real killjoy."

"You'd probably have enough left over for other things too..."

"Like what?"

"Well... I..."

"Say it." Maria said firmly.

"A wedding," Grant said.

"Much as I like you, Grant, I'm not quite ready to get married yet," she said. "I want a proper wedding as well, not one of those late afternoon quick jobs that Alex and Rebecca had."

"Well, we can pay for a proper wedding..."

"Grant, shut up and kiss me, will you?"

****

Zug Station was a military operated outer-system hub for mining ships operating in the Helvetios Kuiper Belt; a place for them to refuel, unload their ore into larger transports and for their crew to relax with each other; the permanent population of just under a thousand was supplemented by around the same number of temporary residents.

As space stations went, it was unremarkable; a large, centralised habitation area with docking arms sticking out of it like some kind of pin cushion and a long downwards tower with an icosahedron shaped object at the bottom.

The latter contained the station's main nuclear fission reactor. Nuclear fission was the norm for any station, base or vessel that was unable to use solar power due to being too far from any star. It did not require the constant input of fuel and high temperatures of fusion, something that was not always achievable with limited resources. If the reactor was in danger of doing a Chernobyl, then it would be ejected into space.

The occupants of that station did not know, but they were about to have the most dramatic month of their lives.

****

Sunita was not planning to go on the station. They had more important work to do as they approached the facility just above the belt, still in hyperspace. Her main job was assessing any new contacts to determine if they were a threat to the ship. As a result, she was sitting in front of the radar screen, which was your fairly standard computer display that showed the contacts and provided information about them.

Once they returned to normal space, their relatively low-powered active sensors would sweep the space around them.

She would need to marry up the data with their passive sensors, including a telescope operated by Fire Officer Louisa Landry, her cornrow wearing deputy. Much of that was done semi-automatically, but the telescope would still need to be pointed at any contact.

You could not necessarily guarantee precisely where you arrived in any hyperspace jump; natural drift could occur, and you could end up a billion kilometres or more from your target. The calculations had set an aim point well above the Kuiper Belt to avoid the risk of any collision.

"Exiting hyperspace in twenty seconds..." David Forgan said. "Everyone strap in please."

Sunita moved to secure herself with the four-point harnesses. The transition could be a little bumpy and even nausea inducing unless you were used to it.

"Strapping in," Sunita said.

"Exit portal being generated... now..." Forgan said.

Vanessa Widomski was sitting in the Captain's chair of *Tulyar*, wearing the white cap that designated any commanding officer on a New London ship. Sunita could see her ticking items off a checklist.

Her Captain was very insistent about following checklists, as she felt a skipped step could lead to disaster. They had been more relaxed on that as an independent ship. Sunita had not liked the new working practice to begin with but was now getting used to it.

A flash in fact of them, reduced to safe light levels by the window filters, appeared, tearing a hole in the redness of hyperspace to reveal a black gap.

"Exiting hyperspace in five, four, three, two, one..." Forgan counted down.

There was a slight downward jolt as they entered normal space and Sunita felt a tiny bit of nausea that went within two seconds.

"Exit complete." Forgan reported.

"Excellent, Mr Forgan. Mrs Kumar, will you activate the radar please," Vanessa ordered. Sunita pressed the key to do so.

Sunita would need to call out the contacts that were appearing on her screen. *Tulyar* lacked an integrated AI system that could say them out loud and respond to further instructions; with the vast array of human (and non-human) voice patterns out there, they weren't generally used on larger or military vessels because of their tendency to misunderstand commands in a crisis.

"We have seventeen contacts. Skunk-1 is a Laguna-Salyut class mining station, identifying as Zug Station. Range 1,900 kilometres bearing Zero-Three-Four Papa Zero-Zero-Four."

Papa and November referred to the bearing above or below the ship respectively; you needed to think in three dimensions in space.

We came out pretty close then, Sunita thought, then continued.

"Skunk-2..."

Vanessa turned to Sunita.

"I know the rules are call out all contacts, but there's seventeen ships out there. Are you doing this to be funny?"

"Yes, Captain!" Sunita said and then giggled. "I'll skip to the good part."

"Please do."

"Skunk-11 is transmitting as Tango-Echo-Whisky-Alpha-Romeo-Four-Five-Nine. Range 1,925 kilometres, Zero-Three-Six, November Zero-Eleven."

TEWAR-459 was a transmitter code for a Terran Union warship; Sunita knew those were not assigned to a fixed vessel for operational security reasons.

She paused and hit her intercom to speak to Landry in the telescope room.

"Landry, get a visual on Skunk-11, please?"

They waited for a few seconds as their optical telescope swung around. She knew Landry was going to start the adjustments needed on the camera to get an image could enough to display on their screen; that would take about thirty seconds. In the meantime, there were other ways.

"We're looking for a *Personality*-class survey ship, hull registration TU-SU-5614. It's a long cylindrical grey ship, with three engines, a large hangar bay on the bottom and more metal on the front than Widomski's high school photograph," she said, deciding to fulfil the other part of her job description as ship jester.

The Captain scowled.

"I never had braces, Mrs Kumar."

Sunita made a wry smile.

Guess the Captain just has naturally good teeth then.

"Looks like it," Landry said. "Can't see the number from here, but it's definitely a *Personality*. What is one of those doing here? This is a very surveyed system."

"Don't know. Possibly coming back from a re-fit. Those aren't new vessels by a long chalk," Sunita replied.

Sunita raised the microphone on her headset and turned her seat to face her Captain.

"Looks like the vessel we came to meet. Suggest we plot course for a docking at Zug and call them up."

"Agreed. O'Hanlon, we're close enough for real-time video communication. Call them up."

****

Daniel O'Hanlon, Communications Officer, started to make a video call to the Terran survey ship. The display in front of him would be relayed to Captain Widomski's own console, allowing for both of them to take part in the conversation. A video call also saved him from having to make a full identification.

The text on the screen showing the connection being made was replaced with a Terran Union Navy crest showing a short-haired brunette in a black coat, her hair blown by an invisible wind. Above lay the name of the ship and a motto:

TUSS Emilia Plater

SU-5614

Z mojej własnej woli

The image was then replaced by that of a short grey-skinned creature with long fingers and large pointy ears that some might call a goblin. Those people would then get yelled at for being racist.

"Greetings, friends," came the sibilant voice of the blue jacket wearing Wilt, humanity's closest neighbours who hailed from the star system once known as Vindemiatrix. It was now called Glafir, a close approximation of the Wiltian traditional name.

"We're here to see Captain Dirk." Daniel said, giving him the standard honorific for any commander of any military interstellar vessel – something not true for civilian vessels.

"You're looking at him," came the reply, as a bony finger tapped a three-stripe rank slide indicating the rank of Commander in the Terran Union Navy, complete with the silver diamond badge of a Starship Commander.

Daniel covered his mouth.

"I'm sorry, I was expecting..." he replied rather embarrassed at the faux pas. He had not even bothered to look at the insignia.

"A human, yes... I get it all the time. Don't worry about it..." the Wilt said, waving the matter away.

"We're the freighter that's here to assist you with this operation. The hospital ship will be joining us at some point," Daniel continued. "We were told to meet you here and then we'll take a short hyperjump over to the current location of the Generation Ship."

"Yes, I was expecting you," Captain Dirk added. "We'll need to calculate our jump settings; I'll get my navigator to discuss that with your own. Anyway, do you have a shuttle?"

"We have two," Vanessa added.

"Doesn't a *Starworker* class have four?"

"Up to four. We're short two."

"Well, send one over please. With you and your security chief please."

"Aren't you docking at the station?" Daniel asked.

"Negative. We've just undocked, and it would be a bit weird for us to go straight back," Dirk replied.

"Roger that."

Guess we won't be docking after all, Daniel realised, *so we will save on the parking charges.*

****

Sunita and Vanessa were sitting in the seating area of their second shuttle, *Walnut M13*, as Maria Penzance, who had just completed her initial apprenticeship and shuttle pilot training, was starting the undocking from *Tulyar,* and setting up for an automated docking with *Emilia Plater.*

"Disconnecting power connection... power connection disconnected," Maria said as she ran through the checklist for an undocking and departure from the port aft shuttle bay. Tulyar had two double bays that could be split or combined as needed, but only two shuttles, with no plans to get any more. Sunita was fine with that; they could use the other one as a basketball court.

Vanessa had put on her full blue New London Merchant Navy uniform, a touch of make-up and her smartest glasses, which went well with her pinned back neck length hair. Sunita, who had merely brushed her hair, well, the wig she was wearing, and straightened her jumpsuit, found herself thinking erotic thoughts about her captain for the second time that day.

Vanessa did not much talk about her private life, but Sunita had easily clocked the wedding ring. She had done some asking around and found some more information before they had left New London. Vanessa Widomski was one of the Proxima Widomski clan, a granddaughter of George Widomski, late lord of the

Proxima mining trade and famously fertile man with fourteen children via five women.

Vanessa had been married to a Derek Sidle, who had died from Acute Radiation Syndrome after a bunch of pirates put him in an exposed compartment while in a high radiation area. ARS was a horrible way to go as your body was ravaged by radiation and your cells so damaged painkillers did not work.

There was a daughter, Anna, from the ten-year marriage, now nineteen and studying at the elite Offaly Starship Academy.

The murder of her husband had resulted Vanessa having some form of psychological breakdown and committal to an institution for a while, but the details were under court seal. At that point, Sunita had decided not to pry any further.

All checks completed, she thought as Maria ticked the final item.

"You may undock, Maria," she said and felt the clunk as they did so.

She looked at the folder that she had printed out for the briefing. With no internal gravity in the shuttle, it was held down by Velcro, each page held securely in its rings to avoid giving the Captain a paper cut on her face.

"Since there's no record of this vessel on the databases, I had to pull design schematics from the common types of the period, Captain," she said. "Once we get close enough, we can identify which type it is and work accordingly. However, it seems to be first generation – not second.

"How can you tell?" Widomski asked.

"All the beacons have an element that shows the human population at the time that they left Sol in binary form. Our one says 8.23 billion... which places it around 2099... which is confirmed by the second element. There's a Julian date as well. 2487814. Which translates to 20 April 2099."

"That date means something..." Widomski observed.

"The day of the Third World War. Humanity, or rather a racist lunatic named Ava Rice, caps off a century of rising temperatures, natural disasters, political upheaval and epidemics with that..." Sunita trailed off as she sensed some disapproval from her boss.

"I know my history, Kumar – I minored in it at the Academy and wrote a dissertation on the Crisis Century. Lucky them, leaving when they did. You had any thoughts on who we're taking on board?"

Sunita brought up a document showing the photographs of the crew. The first of them was the Second Officer.

Vanessa should know all their names by now, but it's good to remind her. Even I mix some of these people up on occasion.

"Yes. Becky Carrington. Her religious community uses a rather archaic English for their scripture, something called the King James Bible. She could probably act as a translator if need be, but I'm not sure how well she could handle a full conversation. We might have to try though."

She moved over to a picture of a tanned man in his thirties with short blond hair.

"Otto Elven as shuttle pilot. We're likely to need to dock manually and that's a tricky thing to pull off when the vessel itself wouldn't be sending standard data feed."

A bearded Latin man holding a wrench and grinning came next.

"Joaquin Lugar, our Deputy Engineer, is rather comfortable in confined spaces and with relics, like this ship is going to be."

"That's four. Who's five?"

"One of our medical team. Probably Hannah Wilmslow."

Kumar did not need to show her Captain that picture; Hannah Wilmslow, a slim red-haired woman in her forties was the ship's doctor and instantly recognisable. Especially when she was doing your monthly medical and tutting about your weight gain.

"Agree to all of them," Vanessa replied.

Sunita looked out of the window at the approaching Terran survey ship. It had its running lights on and a fresh coat of haze grey paint.

"Seems to be a nice ship. For the military, that is."

****

The pressure in the airlock equalised and the inner door opened. Captain Dirk stood in his uniform front of them with a Terran Space Marine guard towering over all the others present. The TSM guard, clad in black uniform with a light vest with a submachine gun slung over his shoulder, was an Elden, a tall, pale species who were reliant on animal blood for their haemoglobin and had pronounced fangs for direct extraction... although doing that was not polite in mixed company.

"Captain Vanessa Widomski, requesting permission to come aboard."

"Sunita Kumar, coming on board," Sunita said as she stepped over the bulkhead in ignorance of standard social conventions.

"Permission granted," Dirk said after a quick eye roll.

Vanessa then stepped over the bulkhead and into the light blue main ship corridor as Captain Dirk retrieved a pot of live worms from his pocket. He offered them to Sunita and Vanessa.

"Wriggler?"

"No, thanks," Sunita said, showing a bit of disgust before checking herself.

"More partial to dead beetles, but thanks for the offer," Vanessa added.

"There's three Wilt ship commanders in the TUN now. George Dirk is my human name, because my own is a bit hard for you humans to pronounce. Except for those who use clicks in their speaking. Anyway, shall we go to my quarters?"

****

Captain Dirk led them to his cabin, which was made up of three small rooms. The key area for them was a restaurant booth style table and seating with a holographic projector in the centre, with various documentation strewn around the centre. Waiting for them was a blonde-haired European human wearing a white lab coat with naval rank slides. She was in her early fifties with a long nose and blue eyes, which she hid behind black rimmed glasses.

"Greetings, Captain Widomski and Mrs Kumar," she said, looking up briefly. "I'm glad you could make it."

"And you are?" Sunita asked.

"Doctor Natalie Anvers." The name that Sunita had been given matched up.

"*Lieutenant Commander* Anvers is my Science Officer," Dirk explained. Sunita saw Natalie bristle slightly at this. Some folks did not like military ranks at all, she knew that being one of them. While she was herself a Warrant Officer in the New London Merchant Navy, being addressed exclusively as Mrs Kumar meant she rarely was reminded of that fact.

"In any event, I'm going to be the science lead on this contact. I have a doctorate in linguistics and another in xenobiology. I think the former will be most useful here. Galactic Standard Manglish is a bit different to pre-space English and you'll need someone to translate accurately. A lot of the key words are the same, but some of their meanings have changed along with spelling and occasionally pronunciation. Could have been worse, at least we didn't have a vowel shift."

Sunita nodded. Manglish was the primary language used across human space. Everyone in human space was taught it in school if not brought up with it. As the name implied, it had considerable influences from Mandarin and used some of its characters in certain short words.

"You know pre-Space English?" Sunita asked. "Seems a niche language to know."

"A profitable niche. Lot of aliens want to read classic Terran literature and translating from the original text allows for the meanings to remain more authentic. My version of *Who's Afraid of Virginia Woolf* is highly in demand."

Sunita decided to change the subject.

"Have we hailed the ship yet?" Sunita asked. "Said 'Welcome to the human race' and all that?"

"Not yet," Dirk said. "I want to do that on closer approach. They're possibly aware that the system is inhabited from our radio overspill, but they won't know anything specific."

"Also, probably not the best idea to introduce them to Wilts at this stage. They've got enough problems getting used to humans without introducing goblins to the equation."

Sunita grimaced and realised that she had put her foot in it.

"Good thing we won't have any then," Dirk sneered.

"Sorry, no offence," Sunita said quickly.

"None taken," Dirk said and then relaxed.

Surprisingly tolerant, Sunita thought, *but then he knew that I wasn't doing it intentionally.*

"In any event, we do not know how far from the ship we will be when we drop out of hyper," Vanessa reflected. "We could be 100,000 kilometres away – or half a billion."

Both vessels could travel through the same portal, but you had to watch your spacing.

"And of course, we'll be dealing with a vessel travelling at 9% of the speed of light... well, I'm glad I'm not the navigator. Rather not collide with that ship. Five hundred years and dying just as they arrived. That would be a real Morrisette moment" Sunita said, then chuckled at her own joke.

Vanessa gave Sunita a disapproving glance.

"And I'm glad you're not the lead contact here," she said, "so let Doctor Anvers do the talking, please."

****

The two ships dropped out of hyper near to the projected point that *Rosa Parks* was going to be. At this point, Helvetios was still the brightest object in the sky, but with an apparent magnitude of -13.5 or so, it was just a very bright moon, relatively speaking.

While they were well outside the range of the star's stellar wind, this part of space was not completely empty – there was a large cloud of hydrogen crystals nearby, ejected from Helvetios in a coronal mass ejection and now frozen.

But *Tulyar* was not there for the hydrogen cloud, of course.

****

"Carrington get our bearings," Widomski ordered. "Landry, let's find the ship."

She pressed the button for the voice communication with *Plater*, which was close enough to make that possible with minimal lag.

"*Plater*, this is *Tulyar*," Vanessa began. "We're doing a search for the vessel now. I am assuming it is still transmitting the Arecibo beacon, so we'll use that to triangulate its position if it's not close enough to be found on…"

Sunita raised her hand.

"Hang on a second," Vanessa continued.

"Found it," Sunita reported. "Friendly-1 is 70,200 kilometres, One-Six-Five-Papa-Zero-Zero-Three... and heading away from us at about Celestial Zero-Nine-Four. Deacceleration about nine metres per second.

Their target was running at just over nine percent of light speed, whereas they were running at a couple of thousand metres a second.

Good thing both of our ships have inertial dampeners, then, Vanessa thought, *because interception's going to take a while. Probably a good fifteen hours at least – we're running at one hundred gravity. Make that ninety because we need to keep the other ship with us.*

"Suggest we plot in a course and then try to contact them. Landry is going to take a picture on the scope once we match speeds," Sunita continued.

"Go ahead. Carrington, please set us up an intercept to be executed on my mark. O'Hanlon call up *Plater* and ask them to contact the ship. They must have seen that if anyone is awake."

****

Sitting at the Communications Console on *Emilia Plater*, Natalie Anvers took a deep breath and started to type her message. The fundamentals of radio transmission had not changed over the centuries, but much of the language had over time, and some of the transmission codes most certainly had. Since the ship was still transmitting on Morse (a method only used by hobbyists), she decided that she was going to use the same method.

The single metal key was a long-disappeared museum piece; she would type her message via keyboard, and it would be sent over at her instruction.

ROSA PARKS, ROSA PARKS, ARE YOU THERE?

There was going to be a bit of a time-lag due to the distances involved, but that was the norm in this business. They were currently eighty-three million kilometres apart and this would increase to over half a billion kilometres before *Tulyar* and *Plater* had matched speeds about eight hours from now. At the former distance, it was going to take four and a half minutes for her signal to reach *Rosa Parks* – and that would expand to nearly half an hour at maximum range.

She pressed the button to send her message and the screen confirmed transmission.

Now, she would just have to wait for the response... and she was then going to have to make a lot of explanations.

****

It had been nearly an hour since they had sent the initial contact message. They had collectively decided to wait an hour before sending a second message to allow their target to process what must be an amazing discovery for them.

Anvers was looking at her language resources when a reply came in, a beep on the screen notifying her of its arrival. She quickly opened the message and read it.

UNIDENTIFIED HUMAN VESSEL, THIS IS ROSA PARKS. WE ARE HAVING A BIT OF TROUBLE COMING TO TERMS WITH THE FACT WE'VE FOUND ANOTHER HUMAN VESSEL OUT HERE. WE DIDN'T EXPECT TO FIND ANYONE ELSE EVER.

Natalie Anvers was not surprised here. They had clearly got an automated burst transmission system on board due to the length of the reply. Short 'telegram' style speech was only something you used when transmission rates were limited (like the Beacon Network) or the cost per word was high. Not something that applied here.

She wrote her reply.

WELL, WE'RE HERE. WE DETECTED YOUR ARECIBO BEACON FROM WITHIN THE SYSTEM. WE'VE GOT A COLONY HERE... AND IN ANY EVENT, THERE'S A LOT OF CATCHING-UP FOR US TO DO. WHAT YEAR IS IT FOR YOU?

****

With 17 hours to kill, Sunita finished her shift on the bridge. She had a thirty-minute chat with Becky Carrington about her sex life and made some suggestions on how she could be more varied in that department, before they had engaged in some further research together on Generation Ships.

After that, she played with her baby daughter, trying, and failing to get her to say "apple", as well as walking her do a bit of assisted walking.

The presence of a baby on *Tulyar*, a not uncommon practice in the Spacee world, had raised several eyebrows with the New London Merchant Navy, with the matter running up all the way to Merchant Admiral Sir Eleanor Cortez, the Chief Executive of the organisation. Sir Eleanor had decided that Kimmy could stay on the ship under *careful* supervision for the current trip to Terra, after which one of her parents would need to stay planet side with her and ensure she was properly educated etc.

Sunita had already decided that her husband would be the one doing that. She just had not told him yet.

****

After seven hours of sleep, Sunita woke up, then engaged in a vigorous spot of early morning exercise with her husband.

She was in the shower when her console rang. She wrapped a towel around herself and staggered over, then pressed the video button in error.

Captain Widomski raised an eyebrow and Sunita blushed before switching to audio. For one thing, she still had shampoo in her stubby hair.

"Er, sorry, Captain," she said. "I wasn't expecting..."

"It's fine, I've seen worse. At least you're wearing *something...*"

"Captain..." Sunita said, looking more flustered. "This is a bit awkward, so can we get to the point?"

"We most certainly can," Vanessa continued, her voice turning business-like. "We matched speeds about three hours ago and Landry was able to get a long-range scope. She estimates it's about a kilometre long. I'll send over the image so you can look, ID the class etc. Call me back when you're decent... better still, meet me in my Day Room. Widomski out."

The image displayed on Sunita's screen. She had seen a couple of generation ships as orbital museums and others in books, but seeing a live one in the flesh...

It was a long tub of a ship with two large engines on the back, various stubby wings and a pointed section at the front that would host the cryogenic pods... of which about a quarter were missing. The hull was probably pocked with micrometeorite strikes, and it was clear even from this distance that this ship was in a bad shape.

But still, it was a find for the ages, Sunita thought.

"Wow, it's actually on the screen... a proper Generation Ship," she said, then turned to her husband lying in bed behind her. "Dan, come take a look at this."

Daniel got up, not bothering to put anything on. Sunita was used to this... but she was going to have to put a stop to it once Kimberley was fully walking.

I am not quite ready to explain the birds and the bees to my daughter, thank you.

He placed a hand on her wet shoulder.

"I know a few scrap dealers who would pay a good deal to tear that apart," he remarked idly.

She glared at him and smiled.

"Bend over, darling, I'm giving you a spanking for that," Warrant Officer Kumar replied.

"Yes, ma'am!"

****

Captain Widomski was sitting in her Day Room when Sunita entered. Becky Carrington, dressed in a long white, full-sleeved dress with lace fringes and sensible shoes was sitting on one of the chairs, with a smile on her face.

"Morning, Sunita," she said.

"Morning, Captain. Becky."

"Morning, Sunita," Becky replied. "Thanks for the tips."

Vanessa looked between the two of them and then laughed.

"No, I'm not giving you a raise for taking on an extra role as a sex therapist... anyway, I've got Natalie Anvers on the line here. She's been talking to the Generation Ship over the course of the night."

Vanessa reached over and took the call off hold.

"Well, I've had a chat with them. Via text as we're not yet close enough for voice," came the voice of Natalie Anvers.

"What did they say?" Sunita replied.

"A bit confused and surprised over the fact we managed to get this far ahead of them, but they seem to be understanding of the situation. They want to arrange a meet and greet. Once we're in range, about nine hours from now, one shuttle from each of us is going to dock with the colony ship. We'll have to make a manual docking as our computer systems are completely incompatible with theirs."

"Indeed. When did they leave?" Sunita asked.

"2099, as the beacon suggested," Natalie replied. "Just after the nuclear exchange, which they saw from their ship as they left... With time dilation on their end, it's 2601 for them..."

Sunita nodded. Time dilation was something that could be noticeable even on shorter journeys. Over long distances, the 'fast-forward' effect would be huge.

"And 2619 for us... but that's likely to be among the least of our problems," Sunita reflected.

"Exactly. I managed to identify the type. It's one of the Galactic Space examples," Natalie said, jumping the gun on the ship manufacturer identification. Sunita had gone over it with Becky herself.

"My guess too. The broad schematics are available on our databanks, but we'd have to request a fuller one from Sol... I know enough for us to get around, but not enough for us to win a game of hide and seek," Sunita responded. "It doesn't look in great condition that's for sure."

"It's a five-century old ship that's not had any overhaul since it left. We're going to have to do an analysis on the various systems, but I'm amazed it's managed to get that far with as little damage as it has. The Space Records Administration are going to want the flight log... that'll be a priceless artefact."

****

The message from Helvetios arrived at Terra's Hyper Beacon at 1104 UTC and was then relayed to the main headquarters of the Terran Union Colonial Office in Lagos, where the cipher server took an hour to decrypt it.

Secretary Jacob Radlett was just about to settle down to a late lunch two hours later when his Chief of Staff knocked on the door. The Chief of Staff looked ashen with shock... and his suit was streaked with dust.

"Secretary, we've received a message from Helvetios. I'll summarise for you, but we appear to have found a missing Generation Ship. Name of *Rosa Parks.* I did a search in our central database and I got told to contact the bank across the street. Apparently, some records were stored there."

That explains the dust, Radlett deduced, *but why hasn't the man cleaned himself up before addressing his Secretary?*

"Mbeki, that isn't unusual. Many colony ship records were historically stored in secure underground facilities and on paper. Anyway, a Generation Ship? First one in about thirty years..."

Radlett realised that his Chief of Staff was looking shocked for another reason and let him continue.

"Sir, it was the nature of the records that I found that most concerned me. The ship wasn't recorded on the standard databases that the archives have - because of who was on board."

"Who? It must be someone scary." Radlett took a bite of his bread.

****

Chief of Staff Albert Mbeki had walked across the street into the branch of Swiss Bank and asked to see the

Manager. As a senior government official, he had plenty
of reason to be there to deal with the currency plates in
the accounts of the Colonial Office. He was shown to
Max Govan's office.

"Good morning, Chief of Staff," Govan said,
bowing for a major client and indeed personal friend.
"How can I help you today?"

"Manager Govan, I need access to Box 28 in Vault
19," Mbeki said as he looked down at his notes. "The
passphrase is 'Berchtesgaden is rebuilt'."

Govan pulled his collar slightly.

"Well, this way, sir."

They had gone down into the sub-basement. Govan
took out his master key card, inserted it into the slot,
and submitted to the retina scan.

The large room had an array of incredibly old, very
solid looking drawers and three doors leading off it.
Mbeki saw the numbers written on them... and that
there was indeed a separate door for number 28.

He pulled out the solid metal key that he had found
in a filing cabinet in his own offices. The record on
Rosa Parks had told him where it was located, which
meant they would not have to drill the lock.

He then inserted it in the slot and turned it four
rotations, a click indicating the door was unlocked.

"I'll leave you to this, Chief of Staff," Govan said.
"Please let me know when you are done."

Mbeki shook his head.

"No, please stay, Manager Govan. I'm genuinely intrigued as to what is in this. Concerned too, considering that passphrase. It was a tyrant's residence in the 20th century."

Govan said nothing.

"Right, let's open this."

It required some force to open the door; both had to pull on the handle to get it open.

Mbeki stepped inside a dark room with an array of cardboard boxes stacked around a table and a video display on the opposite wall.

The air was thick with dust... and then the video display started up. An old, dual heritage, man in a dark grey suit appeared, along with the time code of 11:14 am 04.07.2101.

"If you are watching this, a serious situation has befallen humanity.

My name is Evhen Baransky. I am the President of the United Earth Government speaking to you from the year 2101."

Mbeki recognised the man. Nearly all of humanity would.

The video ran for eight minutes, but the two of them to pause and rewind to follow over bits that they had not caught the first time, as the narration was in a simplified but still archaic English, although someone had thoughtfully provided subtitles in modern Manglish.

When it stopped, Mbeki and Govan turned to each other.

"That," Mbeki said, "is almost certainly the biggest secret in the entirety of human history."

"Do you think *Ava Rice* is still alive after five centuries?" Govan asked. "The Butcher of Humanity survived?!"

"I think that's a very realistic scenario. Now I must go and brief my boss... then, Max, I suggest we find a bar and get very drunk."

Chapter 3

"Ava Rice. The biggest killer in human history is very possibly alive and on-board *Rosa Parks*," Mbeki confirmed.

Radlett needed the Heimlich Manoeuvre. Once Mbeki had done this and he had stopped choking, the Secretary picked up the telephone to call the Ministry of Defence.

"I have an urgent message for Marshal Geri Wald at Special Forces. Tell her that a bunch of Nazis – yes, Nazis – have turned up on a colony ship in the Helvetios system, and she needs to get some Airlock Kickers down there. Ava Rice may be on board. No, I am not making that up. You also need to inform whoever needs informing at Helvetios. FLASH BeaconGram. Correction, ULTRA FLASH."

Radlett hung up.

"After five centuries, do you think that she would still be alive?" he asked.

"Considering those pods and the power systems on those ships were designed for a thousand years, yes sir," Mbeki replied.

"You ever go out to Memorial Park, Albert?"

"Sometimes, Mr Secretary."

"It would be nice if we could actually put the woman responsible for killing three and a half million Lagosians on trial, wouldn't it?"

****

Twenty minutes later, Sunita and Becky Carrington, both clad in their white interior atmospheric suits complete with helmets, were sitting in *Walnut M13* as Otto Elven was making the 40-kilometre journey over to *Rosa Parks. Lambda Sierra* was going ahead of them from the military ship.

All three main ships were travelling 'stern' first as *Plater* and *Tulyar* had needed to slow down to match their speed; the two contemporary ships were the top of a V formation. With all the engines now off for the time being, they were still travelling towards Helvetios at around 27,000 kilometres per second.

In the front, with Becky's help, Otto was conducting a voice call to make the docking possible. Connection would have to be done with an extendable magnetic clamp. This was a common procedure in space operations – although it was generally only done for salvage or emergencies.

Sunita was rather excited. Apart from the two shuttle pilots, the eight of them were serving as the first humans these people had come face to face with for over five centuries. There was so much to discuss.

When the shuttle had attached itself to the hull of *Rosa Parks*, Sunita and Becky would enter the rear airlock and cargo area – a sealable internal door was fitted to *Walnut* for EVA work, unlike the older *Lavender* shuttle that had been lost on Desolation. They would proceed to open the exterior door of *Rosa Parks* and make their way inside, where a reception committee was going to be waiting for them. Wilmslow and Joaquin would follow next once they were inside.

"Two kilometres to docking," Otto said. "Relative speed is ten metres per second..."

Sunita was not one for the finer points of spaceship piloting – all the numbers flew over her head – but she knew that they would have to make contact at a maximum of half a metre per second for the magnets to work properly.

In any event, all she could do now was wait and look out of the window, trying to take in the whole thing. Three layers of glass slightly distorted the image, but not by much.

Rosa Parks dwarfed *Tulyar* but was still smaller than a lot of the space stations that she had docked at over the years.

To think that's a ship we used in our first journeys into the stars, she reflected. *This is a story I will tell my grandchildren.*

****

The time passed slowly. Sunita remembered what Einstein had said about relativity and continued to look at the spaceship.

This will have scientists talking for decades.

As they got closer, Sunita could see that much of the metal on the ship was pitted. Any paint on the side of the ship had long since flaked off. An automated repair bot was attached to the side of the ship, welding a patch to the hull.

"Fifty metres," Otto said. "Turning to dock."

Becky relayed that message as Otto rotated the shuttle so that the floor was pointing in the same direction of the ship's engines, and the rear of the shuttle was pointing towards the hull.

"Docking aligned. Reversing and extending docking clamp."

Sunita could not see the ship now without turning her head to a stupid angle, nor could she see the rear-view camera Otto would be looking at as he made the final approach.

She decided to use the time to decide on her opening words to the people from over five centuries ago. She was not coming over here as a diplomat – the only backside she was prepared to kiss was her husband's one (while she found Captain Widomski attractive, she was not prepared to cheat) – and most of her words would need to be translated, but she would need to interact with the people in any event.

"Forty metres."

Something apt, something pithy.

"Thirty metres."

Something classic?

"Twenty metres."

"Greetings from the human diaspora!"

"Ten..."

Sounds too showy.

"Five... Four..."

"Hi, I'm Sunita. Nice ship you have here."

There was a sharp clang as the magnets contacted the ship.

"Cutting engines. We are secure. Repeat, we are secure."

She felt gravity returning as the ship they were attached to fired up its engines again. Out of the front window, she could see the faint glow of *Tulyar* doing the same, albeit at only a fraction of the power their drives could produce.

Sunita and Becky unclipped themselves from their seats, put on their close-fitting helmets and walked over to the inner door of the airlock. There would be a total of four hatches to go through in order to get inside *Rosa Parks*, so it would be quite time consuming.

Sunita watched as the inner door slid open. She stepped inside and over to the airlock controls, waiting until Becky was inside before setting the controls.

An automated cycle would not work; the area between the two lots of airlocks was currently a vacuum.

"Do I have a good seal on my helmet?" Sunita said. Becky moved over and conducted a visual inspection as Sunita did the same.

"Yes, good seal," Becky replied.

Sunita completed her own examination.

"Good seal on your part too."

Sunita turned back to the controls, adjusting the switches for an automated replacement of the air pressure inside the airlock... then flipped open the cover of the outer door. She slowly turned the handle, and the door began to open, with a strong hiss as the air inside their airlock seeped out into the airtight gap area between the two ships.

Sunita watched as the pressure dropped on the airlock dial and started to increase on the exterior indicator. She started to whistle in her helmet, emitting a tuneless rendition of "Greensleeves."

She heard Becky cough in her headphones and stopped whistling.

"Sorry," she said.

Had my internal microphone on.

After three minutes, the pressure equalised. Sunita then opened the door and the two of them stepped into the connection tunnel. Becky instinctively reached for the door closure switch.

The hatch in front of them was painted a dark red, with the various markings of an external airlock door and the manual handle mechanism in a secure clear plastic box, dented with small holes in it.

"Now it is time for Door Number Three," Sunita said, as she watched that hatch slowly open. What came next was something that neither of them had expected.

Painted on the interior airlock was a swastika and the words:

WELCOME TO GS HORST WESSEL

The two of them looked at each other.

"Er, what's a Horst Wessel?" Sunita asked.

"Don't know. But that's a swastika. Symbol of a genocidal political party..." Becky replied.

Then, the interior hatch opened, and they found themselves facing a dozen jackbooted black uniforms pointing rifles at them. They were all rather Aryan and rather fierce.

Sunita raised her hands.

"I am not going to give this a good review, that's for sure..."

****

Vanessa Widomski was watching their 'prize' rotating its outer wheel when a message flashed onto her console. She read the message and got up.

"I've got a private communication request from *Plater...*" she said out loud. "I'll take it in my Day Room."

Accessing the Day Room was easy; it was literally to the port side of the bridge. She opened the door with her access card and stepped into her office, which she had taken over from the previous Captain.

She had kept it functional, with only a couple of personal touches; a photograph of her late husband, a graduation photograph from the Offaly Starship Academy and a jewelled dagger given to her as an 18th birthday present.

She took her seat, unlocked her console, and pressed the button to make the connection. The face of Commander Dirk appeared. Vanessa's reading of Wilt body language wasn't expert level, but he was clearly showing complete and utter confusion.

"I got an ULTRA FLASH message from High Fleet Command on Terra. A relay ship dropped out of hyper and sent it to me," Dirk said.

"ULTRA FLASH?!" Vanessa said. In terms of message priorities on the Beacon Network, that was the top, reserved only for declarations of war or major emergencies. It would likely be less than an hour old.

"Right... I get a feeling that this is going to be something involving me and my crew," Vanessa replied.

And why didn't we detect the hyper pulse? Vanessa wondered. *Probably they have better sensors.*

"I'll read it out to you. 'Detain Generation Ship Rosa Parks, but do not board – wait for Special Forces. Rosa Parks crew considered armed and dangerous. They are wanted criminals from 21st Century Sol. Commanding Officer of the ship is war criminal Ava Rice. This is not a wind-up. Please confirm receipt.' Now, I've done a crash course in human history and you probably have done a lot more than that."

Vanessa tried to process all of that and instead began blurting out a history lesson.

"Ava Rice?! She's a bit more than just a war criminal. She's *the* war criminal, launched a nuclear war to try to cleanse the planet of those who weren't her type. Killed 2.4 billion people in the process... and destroyed her own country as well. Utterly, utterly mad."

She realised she was almost certainly explaining something that Dirk already knew and put it down to shock.

"Yes, I looked that up. You know, I've never understood intra-human racism. You're all very much alike in my experience."

Vanessa raised an eyebrow.

"That's the sort of attitude that caused so many of our problems."

"Sorry, forgot my cultural training. I mean you're the same physical type in height, overall physical strength, longevity. It's not like us Wilts, who come in all shapes and sizes, more like your *Canis familiaris*. You couldn't confuse me for a Yellow Wilt. Anyway, Rice's apparently dead, but they never found the body."

"Her command bunker was hit by a 2-megaton nuke, there was no body to find."

"Is it possible they made a mistake?"

"I don't... have you told your boarding party about this?" Vanessa asked, her voice now clearly showing her concern as she realised the magnitude of the situation.

Dirk said something that involved a lot of saliva and harsh consonants then broke off the call.

Vanessa moved to make her own call to *Walnut*. She hoped she was not too late.

****

Sunita and Becky raised their hands.

"Becky, would you mind asking these people what they are playing at?" Sunita asked in Manglish.

Becky took a step towards one of the jackboots, who jabbed his rifle towards her. She gulped slightly but decided to continue. She switched to her King James English.

"No, my name is Rebecca Carrington. I am a child of the Lord. Peace be upon you."

The man raised an eyebrow. She realised he was trying to process an English five centuries older than him.

"Who are you? Shakespeare? And who's Fatima here?"

"Her name isn't Fatima. It's Sunita."

"Fatima, Sunita... all the Muslims sound the same to me."

"Becky," Sunita asked, "can you translate please?"

"He thinks you're called Muslim. And that your name is Fatima."

"I think he's being racist."

The man jabbed his weapon at Becky. The word had not exactly changed over time.

"I am not racist."

"Her name is Sunita. We can discuss your attitudes later. Take me to your leader."

"Get the rest of your people out of the shuttle."

Sunita heard the voice of Otto Elven in her ear.

"Sunita, you've not put on your long-range transmitter. What's going on?"

Sunita looked around as Becky heard the request.

"I need to activate my communicator to speak to them, explain what is going on."

At that point, there was a rapid succession of shots coming from somewhere in front of Sunita. She was more gun hamster than gun dog, but it sounded like submachine gun fire.

I think that the military party have just been attacked... and lost. Can't let the others be taken as hostages... Well, I've had a good life...

Sunita then stabbed her communicator herself.

"Otto, emergency departure!" she cried out.

Four seconds passed. One of the goons moved for his rifle. He raised it like a club.

Sunita did not move. He swung.

The rifle slammed into the side of the helmet.

"Sunita!!!" she heard Becky cry as she tumbled to the floor. Her head ringing...

A barked order.

Someone moved towards her, his hands reaching for her helmet.

A hiss as it opened.

A sharp pain on the side of her neck...

"Sunita..."

Blackness.

"If she dies, I'll kill you..."

Silence.

****

Standing in her office, Ava Rice adjusted her cap and looked in the mirror, readying herself for the first physical meeting with whatever was passing as humanity these days.

After nearly five centuries asleep with a yearlong break every century, she knew she would have a lot of adjusting to do. Hyperspace had been something only theorised when she set this stolen ship for the farthest potentially habitable planet on the database. The possibility of humanity coming out here was something she had considered.

It was also one that she had planned for.

Chapter 4

On board *Tulyar*, Vanessa Widomski had walked onto the bridge and via Daniel had made three attempts to contact *Walnut* when Commander Dirk called; *Emilia Plater* was not affected by the jamming due to being at the other top point of the V formation.

"They've activated a rather crude broad-spectrum jammer. Short range but effective. I can try to hop frequencies to my shuttle, but I get maybe half a second of datalink before I lose it again," Daniel said. "We're not an ECCM capable ship."

Louisa Landry raised a hand and Vanessa turned to her.

"Captain, *Walnut* is undocking!"

"Understood."

She got out of her chair and moved over to Louisa Landry.

"Louisa, get the defence team together and meet me in the weapons locker."

****

Outside the forward doors of the shuttle bay, Vanessa Widomski was holding a shotgun in a ready position as they waited for the pressure to equalise in the shuttle bay. *Walnut* had come back and was docked. Daniel was talking to Otto, who had updated them on the situation, but he could easily be lying... and they could be about to face a boarding party.

The light above the door turned from red to green. Maria Penzance pressed the button to open the inner airlock door.

Vanessa moved in; shotgun raised as she saw Louisa Landry entering from the other side. She swung her weapon towards the ramp as it came open, revealing Hannah Wilmslow and Joaquin Lugar.

"What the h..." Hannah said, raising her hands above her red curls. "It's just the three of us."

"Yes. Otto briefed me," Vanessa said. "This day is just getting worse and worse..."

****

Sunita felt the pounding and ringing first, then stale air entering her lungs.

I'm not dead then. Guess my helmet absorbed most of the blow. Plus, someone has taken it off me...

She tried to move her arms... they were tied behind her.

Great. She didn't even buy me dinner.

She opened her eyes, groaned slightly, and raised her head, things now coming into focus.

I think they drugged me as well.

She was in a large control room with many liquid crystal display screens of the sort popular in the early days of the Stellar Age.

A red banner was hanging from the ceiling and she saw Natalie Anvers, dressed in a light blue Terran Union operational suit without her helmet on. She was talking with a very pretty blonde-haired woman dressed in dotted camo with a pistol on her hip. Four armed guards, all men, were standing around the room.

She looked at the display screens quickly, noting that they were still de-accelerating and heading towards Helvetios.

Around 489 astronomical units... well out of the heliosphere for the time being.

She noticed Natalie had blood on her clothing and a split lip herself.

Guess the others are dead. Hope Otto and the others got away.

Natalie spoke up.

"Sunita, you're awake," she said, some relief apparent in her voice.

"Yeah... Where's Becky?"

"She's fine. She's being given a guided tour of the ship," Natalie informed her. "They've been pretty nice to us... well apart from pulling some of our hair out. Not sure what was in aid of."

"That's nice," Sunita replied, slightly confused as well.

Sunita groaned again and then the camo-wearing blonde woman turned towards her, saying something Sunita could only partially decipher due to five centuries of linguistic change.

Sunita felt a sense of recognition of the other woman as she walked towards her, stopping just short and then bending down.

She ran through her mental image directory and came across a name...

Nah, that's stupid...

Natalie paused and then indicated the other woman. "Also, this is Ava Rice."

"Is this a wind up?"

"No, it really isn't."

"This is Ava Rice then?"

"Yes," Ava said. "I am Province Leader Ava Rice. You will show me the appropriate respect for my rank."

Sunita thought for a couple of seconds... then spat in Ava's face.

"Tell her that is for the Guangdong Exclusion Zone," she said, remembering one of Rice's atrocities at random.

At that point, Ava slapped her.

****

Ava Rice walked purposefully away from Sunita Kumar back towards Natalie Anvers, who had been supressing her nervousness and trying to remain calm.

Anvers was a practising Jew, who could trace her family back via Israel and the Netherlands to the Russian Empire nearly eight centuries earlier. She had grown up in a Terran Union where any form of discrimination based on irrelevant criteria like skin colour was a criminal offence and promoting the idea that any form of sapient life was worth less than any other could get you sent to prison. Not that racism was common in the TU at all; she had never experienced any form of discrimination for her religious beliefs or her ethnic identification.

When she had found a book on pre-Space history as a nine-year-old girl and read the section on the Holocaust, she was horrified. Someone had tried to murder her entire people, in a way more akin to slaughtering animals. No, animals were treated better.

And now I am with someone who believes that they did nothing wrong... and then followed up with an even worse act.

Rice stopped two paces from Natalie, then wiped the spittle off her face.

"I guess the South Asians haven't gotten any more intelligent since I left. I'd shoot her for that, but I need some hostages for when your government finally gets in touch with me. What is the name of your government?”

“The Terran Union.” Natalie replied. “President Mohammed Said-Alvarez.”

“A Muslim as leader of humanity?” Rice said, looking slightly perturbed. “A single world government? I clearly failed...

“I made my instructions to Legrand and Konstanz clear! Why did they not act?! Overthrow the soft European Union government and restore a government of the people that would deal with the Islamic threat! It wasn’t hard!”

If Rice loses it, she’s going to shoot me, Becky, Sunita and then finally herself. I need to calm her down... but I’m not going to lie, because she might find out. Well, not too much.

“There isn’t a single government for all of humanity. Sure, the Terran Union controls about 70% of it, but there are plenty of independent systems out there. I’m sure we can find somewhere suitable for you to live,” Natalie informed Ava Rice.

“Live?” Rice raised an eyebrow. “You had a Chinese man on your shuttle...”

“Yes,” Natalie replied. “Well, I suppose you could say he was Chinese.”

Until your men killed him.

"I would need protection as I cannot imagine they would understand the necessary surgery I performed on their country with my pre-emptive strike."

Natalie felt like being sick over Rice's uniform. This was the kind of euphemistic language used throughout history to soften mass murder and she hated it.

"What they don't know won't hurt them," Natalie continued, swallowing the proverbial vomit. "We're the only people that know who you are. A little surgery and a new identity, you and your followers will be able to live their days out on Saxony or New Dakota. Both nice places, great climate, lots of *living space.*"

"Do you have any pictures?" Rice asked, starting to visibly calm down a bit.

"Not on me…"

I mentioned it once, but I think I got away with it…

"What happened to the Chinese and the Africans?"

"All in all, the nuclear exchange you initiated killed around two and a half billion people. I would have to look up the precise breakdown."

Rice grinned.

She's mad. Completely mad!

"Excellent. I did my part of the job, then."

Natalie spat on the floor in disgust.

"You are the biggest killer in human history. Your name is up there with Genghis Khan, Adolf Hitler and Albert Loom," Natalie said, seething. She knew that she was losing it and realised she might need to dial it back.

"Who is Albert Loom?" Rice asked, looking rather intrigued.

"Destroyed the planet Goa IV. Well, not so much destroyed as rendered uninhabitable by crashing a spaceship into it at half the speed of light," Natalie kept her voice as calm as she could.

"What happened to him?"

"He died in the crash," Natalie said.

And it's a real pity that you didn't die in the nuclear exchange.

****

Captain Dirk was sitting on the bridge watching the Generation Ship in the distance. He had no idea how long help was going to take to show up.

He was about to have a bigger problem.

There was a sharp alarm on the screen. A fire control radar was locking onto the ship!

There's no hostile ship... It's the shut...

"Evasive action now!" Dirk screamed, but it was too late. He saw a yellow bolt running from the shuttle's tungsten rod cannon towards his ship.

At twenty kilometres a second. That's a run time of two seconds.

A four-metre-long glowing rod of one of the hardest natural elements slammed through the front cockpit glass.

Straight into him.

He died instantly. This was not the case for the other twelve people around him, none of whom were able to get to their helmets before the bridge depressurised.

****

Vanessa saw two shots from *Lambda Sierra* slamming into *Emilia Plater* – one into the cockpit, the second into the engines – and swore. The shuttle had fired six in total in a broad spread to maximise the chances of a hit. Four had missed, but that was an unimportant point.

"Landry!" she screamed to the sensors console. "Get onto the turret and destroy that shuttle before it fires on us! I'll join you! First Officer Marri, you have the bridge!"

She turned to Daniel.

"Get Grant Robinson to the turret now!"

Then she flipped open the cover over the ship status dial and set it to Red Alert.

****

Louisa Landry quickly left the bridge, closely followed by her captain and heading for the gun turret. She would have a minute to get to the turret before the internal bulkheads were all shut, and after that they would have to be opened manually each time. Not that they were going to take a minute.

She could take out the shuttle, but they would have to get their shots in first before their target could work out how to reload. She had no idea what the reloading time was on that type of weapon and now was not the time to find out.

Landry moved into the red-lit turret's seat, pulling down the binoculars in front of her to see out through the sight. Her hands moved to the turret controls. As a former New London Naval Gunner, she knew how these systems worked.

She heard whirring to her right as Vanessa requested the ion propulsion unit and the heavy metal slug that would be put together to form the cannon rounds. There was room for a second loader on the other side, but Grant was not going to be there for a minute or two, depending on how quickly he got through the doors.

She placed her eyes against the rubber eyepieces, adjusted the focus...

On the display, she could see a green arrow indicating the direction of *Rosa Parks*, which moved as the ship began to roll and move laterally to its right to get a better shot on the shuttle.

She started to swing the turret around, hoping that the turn rate was high enough.

10 degrees a second.

Roughly 160 degrees to move, not counting the need to elevate the turret.

Ten seconds later, a white icon on the right indicated that the right barrel was loaded. The turret continued to move.

The shuttle's turret can move faster, Louisa knew, *but do they have the ammo to spare on us?*

Ten horribly long seconds passed as the turret continued to move closer.

Through the binoculars, she saw *Lambda Sierra* coming into view.

The target indicator moved onto *Rosa Parks...*

The distance changed from infinity to thirty-nine kilometres...

A second clang, the other barrel loaded.

The indicator moved onto *Lambda Sierra* as she saw its own turret align on *Tulyar...*

She pulled the trigger twice, literally giving her target both barrels. The visor display went black to shield her eyes from the ion blast as the two rounds shot out and initiated their engines, rapidly accelerating towards a maximum relative velocity of 150 kilometres per second.

The visor opened again and the last thing she saw, before she was blasted into the rear wall, was the bright glow of a tungsten bolt...

****

Vanessa felt the ship shudder as the tungsten bolt struck home. She herself fell to the floor as the lights went out. She got up as the lights came back on and saw Louisa.

She moved quickly over to her gunner, who was starting to come round... and whose face then turned to panic.

"I can't see! I can't see!" Louisa yelled. "I've gone blind!"

Probably from the concussion, Vanessa thought. Probably temporary. If not, I'm billing the Terran Union for the implant.

She moved to the intercom.

"Bridge, this is the Captain! What's our status?!" Joaquin replied.

"Two clear hits on the shuttle. It's gone."

"Got it. Get Hannah in here now. Louisa Landry is down. Suspected concussion."

****

Sunita felt *Rosa Parks* shudder twice in quick succession.

Then it began to move slightly to the right.

"What was that?!" she screamed. "What the actual flying..."

****

Natalie Anvers also felt the ship shudder. It was a bit hard not to. She saw Ava Rice move over to a console and press a button.

"Squad Leader Lund, Section Leader Abilene!" Rice screamed. "Report please!"

Anvers moved over to Sunita, who was looking rather alarmed while still listening to Rice, then switched to Manglish and a whisper.

"When I was captured, Rice's people were going over the shuttle. They were trying to get the weapons to work..."

Rice repeated her call, then moved to another console. An old video display appeared, showing *Lambda Sierra*.

Or rather what was left of *Lambda Sierra* with a massive hole in the centre of it...

Rice swore in her other first language of German and then changed the display, which showed *Emilia Plater*... with its bridge wrecked, a large hole in the engine and the craft gradually drifting away as it could no longer change its speed.

Oh, b... Natalie thought.

The screen changed again to *Tulyar*, which was showing a wrecked turret.

Rice grinned and then moved to another console.

"Right, I need you to start talking with your merchant ship," she instructed. "Time to give them my demands."

****

Captain Widomski had returned to the bridge just before the radio connection was made. She was looking shaken but still had adrenaline coursing through her.

She heard the soft and melodious voice of Ava Rice that she had only ever heard in documentaries before, then Natalie's translation.

"Look, Captain, I've just wrecked your escort and totalled your gun. You no longer can destroy me, and I have three of your people as hostages. So, I suggest we start talking."

Vanessa seethed inwardly. She thought about being polite and charming, trying to get on this woman's good side. Then, she decided that idea could go jump off a cliff.

"Look, Ava. Can I call you Ava?" she began then carried on regardless. "I may be the Captain of an old but classic space freighter, but my ability and inclination to give you any of what you want was already next to nil.

When you fired on my ship, that went to nil... but you've done something even worse."

Rice fumed.

"Explain!" she barked.

"You fired on a military vessel of the Terran Union. You've probably done it some rather severe damage and killed a few of its crew..."

"That was two people acting on their own initiative against my instructions."

Vanessa rolled her eyes.

Liar. If you didn't order it, you were certainly OK with it. Like all tyrants. And a few seconds ago, you were boasting about it!

"Whatever, my Nazi friend. We know who you are. You're a wanted mass murderer. Not sure how we're going to prosecute you for offences committed five centuries ago... but that's kind of moot. You've committed several acts of murder in Interstellar Space... which means anyone can prosecute you for those, and I'd happily stand in the witness box at your trial.

"In any event, you've really annoyed the Terran Union..."

The voice of Maria Penzance cut in.

"Hyper pulse! Bearing One-Eight-Zero..."

Vanessa Widomski looked at her own display.

"Excuse me, Ava, I need to put you on hold."

Two seconds later, Rosa Parks was regaled with the sounds of the "The Girl from Ipanema".

****

Major Dora Ortega, commanding officer of the Terran Union Marine Corps ship *Margaret Carter*, felt the slight lurch as her ship transitioned into regular space. As it moved clear from the portal and the electrical interference, her active and passive sensor operators started calling out contacts.

Three vessels, running at Celestial Zero-Nine, heading away from her. It would be a good while before they caught up with them, especially with the 75g maximum acceleration on what was a troop transport at its core.

Plenty of time to think up a battle plan though.

"Sir! *Emilia Plater* is broadcasting a distress signal."

Ortega was powerless to help as the intercept course was set in front of her; it would take over 30 hours to rendezvous with the ships closest to her, let alone the stricken survey ship. With the inaccuracy inherent in any short hyper jump, she could not get any closer... and they would still need to match speeds.

She could at least contact them to get a report on the situation, but, as she scratched her eyebrow, she knew that it would just give her something to worry about... but she would still need to call *Tulyar* in any event.

****

"And that's almost certainly the Special Forces showing up," Vanessa replied. "Start confirming that Maria, please."

"How am I going to identify a Special Forces ship?" Maria asked.

"That's a particularly good question. They are hardly going to wave a big sign saying, 'I'm a Special Forces ship'. Hang on, I'll ask Mr Marri."

Darius Marri had been a shuttle pilot with New London Special Forces in a past life. While hardly the biggest organisation in the galaxy – around one hundred personnel in all – they still had some decent skills. He had had been assisting Clarissa Müller, the ship's engineer, in a full electrical diagnostic after the tungsten bolt attack.

She dialled up his personal comm.

"Darius, it's the Captain. When you were flying in Special Forces, how did you disguise yourself?"

"That's classified," he replied. "I'd be breaking the Official Secrets Act if I told you."

Maria sighed. She would clearly need to rephrase this.

"*Without* breaking the Official Secrets Act," she began, "please tell me how a Special Forces ship might disguise themselves."

"Well..." Darius said, more cheerily. "They might either go no transponder... or they'd choose a handle that would tip off any military expert that they were in fact Special Forces if they needed to act covertly."

Maria heard a ping. She turned back, looking at the display and the contact information that had appeared on their new contact.

"Tango Six Dash Two Four One Eight X-Ray. Full name, Transport Ship *Margaret Carter*."

"Yep, that'll be Special Forces. Margaret Carter was a Governor of Terra about a century ago… and before that she was a General in TUSF."

"Not exactly subtle."

"They're not the most subtle of people. I really must tell you about the joint counter-piracy exercise we did with them sometime…"

****

After fifteen loops of "The Girl from Ipanema", Sunita Kumar was losing the will to live. So, she decided to kill someone. Or at least beat them up.

"Hey!" she cried out in pidgin English. "I need to poo!"

She genuinely needed to relieve herself, but it was also a way of getting herself untied.

She saw Ava Rice hear the cry and say something to one of the guards. The guard walked over to her and untied her. Sunita got unsteadily to her feet.

****

Rebecca Carrington had felt the ship shudder twice and almost fell over. Her assigned escort had hit the intercom and been told what was going on by someone.

He told her that there had been a couple of meteorite impacts.

I've been on enough ships to know what a space debris impact is like. That did not sound like a debris impact.

Her escort was named Jimmy. He was a pleasant and charming young man from somewhere called Wisconsin with blond hair, blue eyes, and a square jaw. He also had a machine pistol.

She had been taken from the main control room round to the living area. Jimmy explained that there were currently seventy people on this ship; twenty of whom had woken up from a century of sleep a week earlier to prepare the ship for the arrival in Helvetios.

The rest were still in cryo-sleep.

The living area had been cleaned up, with the dust in situ from a century ago removed. It was fairly Spartan with an array of bunk beds attached to the wall in the bedroom area, along with a large canteen and a recreation room. Becky was rather disturbed at all the posters around. A lot of them were of a man with a toothbrush moustache who she faintly remembered from history class. Others had grotesque caricatures of certain human ethnicities, some bearing the Star of David.

Are those supposed to be Jews? They look nothing like the Jews I've met.

Then Jimmy had offered her some food, namely a baked beans bin with a Best Before Date of "May 2301". She took it for later consumption; it would be an interesting thing to try later...

Now, thirty minutes after the 'collision', she was now clambering up some stairs into an area marked as Hydroponics.

She found herself in a huge tunnel, two hundred metres tall and one hundred metres in diameter. There was a veritable jungle of plants of all types, all mixed... she could not see far into it.

This is what you get when you leave crops growing for five hundred years. They all merged.

"We hope to start harvesting this soon. Give us some fresh food rather than the tinned stuff." Jimmy said.

Becky thought about what she would say. Lying was a sin after all.

"I'm very impressed with the work that you've done here."

She prayed that this tour would be over soon – along with her captivity. She would rather not die here, but of course the Lord might have other plans for her.

****

Sunita had been led by the guard into one of the bathroom areas. After doing her business, she moved over to the sink where a fresh cotton towel was present.

Probably freshly produced from their fabric stores, Sunita figured, *not everything here is going to be five hundred years old.*

She washed her hands.

Then turned towards the guard.

"Hey, Hitler! Think fast!"

With that, she threw the towel at his face.

While white Egyptian cotton covered his features, she delivered a powerful kick to his groin.

He contorted in pain.

Sunita grabbed a liquid soap dispenser.

Then hit him over the back of the head.

He dropped like a sack of potatoes. Blood and soap began to mix on the floor below him.

"Yes! She shoots! She scores!" Sunita cried and picked up his assault rifle, noting that the fundamentals of those types of weapons had not fundamentally changed.

She stepped back into the corridor; her weapon raised. If there were any other armed goons out there, she would need to be the first to fire or she could end up dead.

She did not really want to bet that and hoped that the adrenaline rush would speed up her reflexes when it came to pulling the trigger.

****

Darius Marri had entered the bridge as the first message came in.

Just before he was to take his seat in the sensors console chair, he saw the message on the screen and moved over to read it. Daniel let him look with no objection.

MESSAGE FOR TULYAR & EMILIA PLATER. THIS IS SPECIAL FORCES SHIP MARGARET CARTER. PLEASE PROVIDE YOUR STATUS.

"Captain?" he said. "Do you mind if I handle this conversation? I speak SpecFor much better than you can. And military."

"Be my guest, Mr Marri," Vanessa said and vacated her seat to him. She moved to one side.

Marri stretched out his fingers and started to type.

CARTER, THIS IS TULYAR. IT APPEARS THAT ONE OF PLATER'S TS-13S, LAMBDA SIERRA, WAS TAKEN OVER BY TANGOS WHO USED THE TUNGSTEN REVOLVER ON THE SHIP. I HAVE HEARD NOTHING EXCEPT THE DELTA SIGNAL FROM PLATER, BUT THEY APPEAR TO HAVE TAKEN SEVERE DAMAGE. WE USED OUR OWN WEAPONS ON THE SHUTTLE TO SPLASH IT. IT GOT ONE SHOT OFF WHICH WRECKED OUR CANNON. ONE WIA AMONG OUR CREW. CONCUSSION.

He pressed the send button. The reply came back a minute later.

TULYAR, THIS IS CARTER. YOU EX-SPETSNAZ? YOU KNOW THE LINGO. PLEASE GIVE YOUR FOUR LINE.

"Four Line?" Vanessa asked.

"Name, rank, number, specialisation," Marri replied. "Standard term in the Terran forces. We use Tag Code in New London for it."

DARIUS LINH MARRI, 1ST LIEUTENANT, LG334, SC-9. FIRST OFFICER HERE.

The reply came slightly quicker.

DORA SANCHEZ ORTEGA, MAJOR, 5429413, CT-2. COMMANDING OFFICER.

Darius sighed.

"Dora Ortega. Meat Shield Ortega. Used a dead pirate as a ballistic shield during a zero-G asteroid assault. She's trigger-happy even by Airlock Kicker standards."

Vanessa looked confused.

"You've not heard of TUSF's reputation? They don't even bother with any attempts at negotiation. They'll assault whenever they feel like doing it, even if the cops are close to a peaceful solution."

"I remember that now... I'd just forgotten the nickname for that particular part of them. That sounds... alarming."

"Especially if you're a hostage. It's deterred most pirates from going near TU space, but it's exceedingly difficult to storm any ship quickly enough to prevent hostages dying," Darius continued. "And I'm not sure Ortega is going to care too much about the hostages. She'll take them as a write-off. Acceptable losses."

"This is why, as a Spacee, I hate the military sometimes. If you excuse me, I need to go and have a think," Vanessa replied and left the bridge.

Maria spoke up at this point.

"To be quite honest, I'd be rather happy if they shot Ava Rice. I'd do it myself if I had the chance."

Chapter 5

After an hour, the hold music came to an end. Vanessa came back on.

"Right, Ava baby."

Ava scrunched up her face as Natalie Anvers started to translate again.

"You should have more respect for your leader. I'm the greatest thing that happened to humanity. Killing all those excess Chinese and blacks eased the pressure on humanity's resources."

"If you say so..."

"I do."

"I'm going to make it pretty clear. You've not got a chance against the Terran Union. They'll happily blow your ship to pieces. Your great escape from Earth will go completely untold. Why would they want to admit that you got away?"

Ava looked confused at this. Natalie wondered why.

"Hang on... you don't know do you?"

"Know what?"

"You've been presumed to be dead for the last five centuries. We all thought you died in your bunker after the Chinese nuked it."

"Well... I'm clearly not."

"Well then," Vanessa said, "surrender and you'll have an interstellar audience. You can make your case to all sophont-kind."

Natalie wondered how to translate the word 'sophont'. She went for "all of humanity and their alien friends."

"Can I have some time to think about it? It's a big decision and I need to consult with my fellow Europeans on this."

"You have an hour. I expect to hear from all my people that they are still alive. Any harm comes to them and the deal is off. You will need to talk to the Terran Union instead. Widomski out."

There was a ping from a console. Ava Rice walked slowly over to it and then tapped some buttons, then started to smile with glee.

That doesn't look good.

Ava reached into her holster for her pistol. She raised it slowly and pointed it at Natalie's head.

"You're Jewish, aren't you?"

Natalie gulped.

"How do you know?" Natalie asked. Then she remembered. The hair pulling. Rice had taken DNA samples from each of them.

"I took hair samples from each of you. Ran them through my analyser. Your curry chomper came back as mostly Tamil Indian. Figured that. Shakespeare was heavily Western European with a bit of Pole in her.

"You came back with Haplogroup J-M267. That's pretty common among Jews. Now as you of course know, Jews are a threat. I would have destroyed Israel if I had warheads to spare."

Ava pulled back the hammer. Natalie closed her eyes.

"*Sh'ma Yisra'eil Adonai Eloheinu Adonai echad. Barukh sheim k'vod malkhuto l'olam va'ed...*" she began.

Then the hammer clicked again.

Natalie opened her eyes to see Ava Rice smiling. The woman then placed her pistol on the table and then raised her hands in surrender.

"I accept your captain's offer. I look forward to my trial. It's a pity Hitler killed himself. He never got the chance to make his case."

There were three gunshots and the thud of a body falling to the ground. Then Sunita Kumar burst into the Control Room, submachine gun raised.

"Prepare to die, you Nazi moth... Oh, you've surrendered."

Sunita and Natalie looked at each other. Natalie laughed and then moved over to the chair where Sunita had been tied up, then kicked it over.

"Since you've got the gun," Natalie said, "do you mind covering me while I tie this lady up. Then I'm going to do an all-ship announcement telling people to stand down."

Ava coughed.

"They're not going to listen to any of you lot."

Natalie realised that this excuse for a human female was almost certainly correct.

"Correction, Kumar, that is probably going to come best from Ms Rice here. Tie her hands at the front so she can operate the intercom. If she tries anything," Natalie added, "shoot her in the leg. I want to keep this woman alive."

Natalie Anvers picked up the rope and walked back to Ava.

"Kneel please... Ava Rice, I am arresting you for murder, contrary to Section 20 of the Terran Union Criminal Code..."

I'm not going to mention I have no legal authority to make anything but a citizen's arrest...

****

President Mohammed Said-Alvarez had been on an official visit to Proxima. A brown-skinned man of 74 Terran years, he had spent over ten years as Chief Executive of Humanity, engaging in the usual activities of a head of state on his trip to one of humanity's first extrasolar colonies. Cutting ribbons, greeting high-profile guests, listening to a prodigious amount of waffle, eating rubbery chicken and feigning interest in mining tools.

Now sitting on board *Terra One* in Very High Earth orbit heading for Luna, he was in the middle of some excellent guava juice and reading the latest reports on Operation Cooldown, when he got an ultra-secure call from Secretary Radlett.

Radlett appeared on the video display looking pensive. A display on the screen indicated there was a three-second communication lag on each end due to the distances involved. The President would press a button to indicate when he was speaking, and Radlett would do the same to avoid awkward overlaps.

"Mr President," he began. "Apologies for not being able to brief you before, but you were in transit and this was a matter of urgency. It's to do with the Generation Ship we found yesterday. You were informed of that before you jumped, I believe."

"Yes, that's correct, Radlett. What have you found out?"

"I feel it best to demonstrate via an old video. An incredibly old video. There is a subtitle system present that the caretakers have handily updated."

The video began as Said-Alvarez rubbed his own white beard.

About the same age as me, he observed, *but he's taken less care of himself.*

"If you are watching this, a serious situation has befallen humanity.

My name is Evhen Baransky. I am the President of the United Earth Government speaking to you from the year 2101."

Said-Alvarez knew full well who Baransky was. Once President of Ukraine, he had ended up taking charge of the international union that had formed in the aftermath of the Third World War, literally because his name had drawn from a hat. His calm and effective leadership had stopped even more people dying in the nuclear winter. He was heralded as the saviour of humanity and there was a statue of him outside the Terran Senate.

He was even on the ten-credit note.

Furthermore, Baransky was considered the first Chief Executive of Humanity, the title that Said-Alvarez legally held but chose not to use, finding it pretentious.

Said-Alvarez saw that Baransky looked weary already; his hair was thinning, and he had liver spots on his face. Seven years after this, cancer would claim him.

"I have recorded this message to be seen if the Generation Ship *Rosa Parks* is ever found..."

Said-Alvarez, a man very much in command of policy if not exactly the greatest public speaker in the galaxy, reached for his digital notepad. The slight twinge of pain from his arthritis was swiftly put out his mind as he started taking notes.

Rosa Parks was a newly constructed colony ship about to head for Teegarden's Star as part of the Settlement Fleet... Hang on, we call that place Teegarden these days...

Due to carry two hundred colonists, mostly from Texas-Mexico and the Liberty Republic... had a skeleton crew of ten on board while awaiting their arrival...

Starport facility in Houston was attacked by a group of terrorists and the shuttles were launched without authorisation...

Shuttles then docked with Rosa Parks in geostationary orbit. Killed nine of the crew. Tenth identified Ava Rice then escaped via another shuttle... arriving in West Africa as the nuclear exchange took place. Eventually found his way to Lagos and told his story to the authorities.

In the confusion, Parks fired its engines and was heading away from Sol before anyone realised... heading in the direction of the Pegasus constellation...

Decided to cover up Rice's escape for the sake of human morale... Parks was officially reported as having burned up in the atmosphere, omitted from the main records...

"What you think of our actions is something I cannot know. However, since you have discovered Rice and her associates, I assume you will not wish to see her free to spread her hate. As such, we have put together a large string of documentary evidence testifying to her direct involvement in the nuclear strikes that have devastated much of our planet as well as other crimes..."

The President paused the message and resumed the call with his Secretary.

"Radlett, what am I watching?"

After seven awfully long seconds, his Secretary responded.

"Sorry, what do you mean, Mr President?" Radlett looked confused.

"A video stating that Ava Rice is alive and on the ship that we just found approaching Helvetios. Is this a hoax?"

"The documentation we recovered from Swiss Bank suggests anything but, sir."

"Secretary Radlett, as the media love to point out, I am the supreme executive ruler of just over eleven and a half billion people at the last count. I am, as they also love to mention, therefore the most powerful human being that ever drew breath."

"Yes, sir."

"Then kindly explain, how, *in the name of all that is putrid,* I didn't know about this."

"It appears that everyone involved swore a vow of secrecy, including a family of cleaners who used to come in every few years to check the equipment was working and service some other vaults. The last one of those died just before the turn of the century according to one of the older staff at Swiss Bank. A search back through the archives suggest that there was a brief claim in 2456 that Rice had escaped in... err... *The Fomalhaut Enquirer*. It named the ship in question."

"Well at least there is something funny about this," the President remarked, satisfied with the explanation. "Anyway, is Procurator-General Anvers aware of all this?"

"I've informed him, sir."

"How did he take it?"

"After the shock, some rather considerable glee, sir."

"I bet he'll be wanting to prosecute that case personally."

"I can imagine, sir. He wants to be Governor of Terra and this would give him the perfect platform to base a campaign off."

"That is assuming of course that we take her alive. I somehow doubt that is likely from what I recall of the Nazis."

"I believe a lot of them did go on trial, sir."

"Finally, I don't have much call to go into Christian churches, being a Muslim, but I seem to recall that Evhen Baransky became a saint after he died. Can you revoke a sainthood?"

"I'll ask the Pope, sir."

"He wasn't Catholic. He was Orthodox."

"I'll ask whoever is in charge of them then, sir."

"It's the Ecumenical Patriarch. Name of Stephen. We used to play golf together. Ask him what his handicap is these days."

****

"So, let me get this straight, Mrs. Kumar," Vanessa Widomski said as she sat in the Day Room on *Tulyar*. "The biggest criminal in human history, a woman who brought about the deaths of around 2.4 billion people, has actually surrendered?"

"You did ask her to." Sunita replied over the radio. "She's standing about three metres behind me. Becky Carrington has some ancient submachine gun trained on her. Looking quite h... sorry, that's inappropriate in the circumstances..."

Vanessa ignored that last part.

"I wasn't expecting her to actually do it. I honestly feared that she was going to kill the lot of you, but I was hardly going to assist her. You know my surname, Widomski?"

"It's of Polish origin, isn't it?"

"Yes. Those monsters killed a sixth of the Polish population in the 20th century."

"So, I would not have personally minded if you'd shot her. That would have made our lives a lot easier..."

"We can still..."

"*No.* I will not countenance murder," Vanessa said very firmly. "She is now our prisoner. So, I assume are the rest of the crew?"

"Well, they haven't come storming in here to rescue their messiah, so I assume that they complied with her instructions."

"Her instructions?"

"To stand down and let her leave the ship. Apparently for discussions."

Vanessa thought for a second.

The woman has to save face I assume.

"Right, we'll bring her on board and put her in the brig. *Walnut* is ready to go back over for transport. I am going to instruct that anyone who goes near Rice wears a face mask. I don't want any of us giving her any of our bugs and for all we know she could have Influ-2050 or something like that. Once the medical ship arrives, we can transfer her over to there."

"Understood, Captain. How long will *Walnut* be?"

"Twenty minutes or so. I will confirm. *Tulyar* out." Maria got up.

"Captain, I wish to raise a formal objection to us taking this woman on our ship."

"Ms Penzance. Why are you objecting?" Vanessa asked.

"Because she is a dangerous criminal, and she will almost certainly attempt escape. We are not equipped to be jailers."

"We are most certainly not, but there aren't exactly a large number of other ships around at the moment."

"Transfer her to *Margaret Carter.*"

"They're not here yet... and I am not having her accidentally slip in a jail cell, sustaining a fatal head injury."

"By your own comments, you wouldn't seem to mind."

"Penzance, you are out of line," Vanessa responded. "I command this ship, not you. No harm is to come to her. Do I make myself clear?"

Maria nodded slightly.

"Do I make myself clear?!" Vanessa barked.

"Yes, ma'am."

****

"Wow," Ava Rice said as she stepped into the shuttle. "So, this is 27th century technology..."

"Yes, it is." Natalie Anvers replied.

"It looks rather similar to my technology. More primitive in fact. That monitor looks like something that would be in a museum in my day."

Natalie looked at the monitor.

"That's just the fashion. User interfaces go in and out of style."

Sunita pointed at a jump seat.

"She wants you to sit down."

Ava did so and Natalie secured her in place with the four-point harness. She wouldn't be going anywhere.

A red-haired woman with a medic armband came over to her, handing a small over ear face mask to Natalie.

"I'm Doctor Wilmslow. Medic on *Tulyar*. Please wear that as we don't want to give Ava Rice anything," the woman asked. Natalie complied.

They strapped in and undocked. Natalie felt the zero gravity start to kick in... and so did Ava Rice.

"No artificial gravity?" the Nazi asked.

"Not in a shuttle. Too small," Natalie replied. "Will be on our ship."

"Cool. The future is nice."

In front of her, Natalie saw Doctor Wilmslow examine Sunita, making sure that she was OK after being drugged. She watched the procedure.

"Hey, Mexican!" she heard Ava cry out.

"Sorry, Mexican?" she asked.

"The Mexican at the front."

"Mexican?" Natalie asked, trying to remember her history of Terra. She had not exactly got access to a historical atlas of Earth before the unification.

"Do you not know where Mexico is? Central America? Full of dirty drug dealers with awful music who like to immigrate without getting permission?"

Natalie face-palmed.

****

An hour later, Vanessa was standing inside where *Walnut* had just landed. She had put on her full uniform including peaked cap.

The ramp opened to reveal Sunita and Becky holding Ava Rice, with Natalie Anvers bringing up the rear. They were wearing face masks... and Ava Rice was gagged with a big piece of duct tape over her mouth.

Deputy Engineer Lugar was sitting down typing something and Otto was clearly still in the pilot's seat.

"Mrs Kumar?" Vanessa asked. "Why have you gagged the prisoner?"

"Because she was abusing Joaquin apparently, and I don't want to get 21st Century Disease from her loud talking."

Vanessa nodded.

"Why am I not surprised at any of that? Take her to the brig, inventory her stuff and then join me in my Day Room," Vanessa instructed. "Also, do a full cavity search because I don't want her killing herself."

Sunita winced, obviously at the thought of inspecting a genocidal maniac's private parts.

"Yes, Captain. Do you want me to make a formal arrest as well? As a Security Officer, I have the power to detain her for a criminal offence until she can be passed onto the appropriate authorities. As of course do you."

"Good idea. Cross the legal Ts, so to speak. Dr Anvers, can you translate please?"

"Yes, I can," Natalie replied.

As the three of them went off, Hannah Wilmslow spoke up.

"We're going to go back over to the ship. I want to check everyone out medically if I can and look at the icicles. Get an idea of what the med ship is going to have to deal with," she told her boss.

"You do that, Hannah," Vanessa replied. "Just be careful. Also, ask Dr Anvers to send over some key phrases you might need. Like telling the people on board that if they attack you, Ava Rice dies."

"I thought you weren't going to kill her, Captain?" Hannah asked, looking slightly confused.

"I am not. But they do *not* need to know that."

****

Vanessa had to go through the Bridge to return to her Day Room. As she did, Darius Marri turned the command chair around to face her.

"I've got a message from *Emilia Plater*. Or rather what's left of it," Marri said.

"Let's hear it..." Vanessa said.

"It was from their Marine Chief. Elden guy named Tree Climber Blue. His repair team managed to stop a total depressurisation, but they had to eject the reactor core. The bridge is wrecked, and the ship is a write-off. They're going to use the back-up thrusters to slow themselves down enough to be captured by Helvetios' gravity and head in-system to pod out."

"How many dead?"

"19, including Commander Dirk. Sorry about that."

"A pity, I liked him."

"Another thing," Darius said. "Apparently the Nazis renamed their ship to something called..."

"*Horst Wessel*. No, I'm not sure of what that is either," Vanessa replied.

"I looked it up. It's a man from the 20th century. He was a 'stormtrooper' during the rise to power of Adolf Hitler. Was shot in the head by a Communist and died of blood poisoning. The Nazi Party turned him into a martyr and even named their party anthem after him."

"How charming. We're not going to dignify them by accepting the name. The ship will remain *Rosa Parks* in our reports. That's an order."

"Ma'am, you really don't to need make that an order," Darius replied. We'll happily comply."

Vanessa started to walk towards the door.

"Another thing - allocate Dr Anvers to one of the guest rooms and find her some clothing to wear. I think she's the same size as Clarissa, but double check with her."

****

Four hours later, Doctor Hannah Wilmslow was standing by one of the cryogenic capsules on *Rosa Parks*. She had a submachine gun on her shoulder, something that she really did not like doing as someone who had sworn the Hippocratic Oath. Joaquin was with her, also armed.

It generally took a day to do a proper thaw from cryogenic 'stasis'; fortunately, there were a couple of examples on defrost now. Including one just about to be at serving temperature.

She strained to read the name on this capsule, written in faded writing. Joaquin had a tablet with him and a radio transmitter that meant that he could access *Tulyar*'s databanks.

"Mich... Michael... Michael Garrett!" she said.

Inside the capsule, now nearly free of ice, an old man was lying inside. He was dressed only in underpants and had a prominent beard; while cryogenic stasis slowed bodily processes to near zero, they did not stop them entirely.

Joaquin tapped the name onto the tablet and waited.

The man's eyes opened. Hannah decided it was time to open the lid.

"Hey, hey," she said in 'pidgin' English. "No move. No move yet. You awake now. It is 2619."

She felt a tap on the shoulder and turned. Lugar was showing her the tablet.

Michael Garrett, she thought, *Lead propagandist for the New Confederacy. Wouldn't be surprised if he had some charges to answer... Are they all going to be like this?*

****

"So, what can I expect from my upcoming trial?" Ava Rice grinned from inside the cell.

Sunita Kumar had taken Ava Rice's clothing and other personal effects to the equipment room. Rice had been given a jumpsuit to wear, which she was carrying off with considerable style.

To call it a brig was a stretch. *Tulyar,* like most merchant ships of its type, had a single cell with a bed, sink and toilet, which was designed to hold people who were posing a danger to themselves and/or others. Vertical bars made up three of the walls, giving no actual privacy to the occupant; the curtain around the toilet area needed replacing after a previous occupant had torn it off.

Becky Carrington was sitting on a wooden stool outside the cell. She had changed out of her suit into a long frilly red dress with heavy boots, although she was wearing a face mask as recommended. She also had a shoulder holster with a small calibre pistol inside it in case Ava tried anything funny. If needed to, she could use it and use it accurately; she had shot a lot of vermin on Dom Pennsylvania.

Calling Ava Rice vermin is an insult... to vermin.

"I am familiar only with trials on Dom Pennsylvania. There you would be hanged for your crimes. Not something I personally favour. He that is without sin among you, let him first cast a stone at her."

"The Book of John," Ava sounded curious. "You're a Christian, then? So am I. I was just doing my duty to protect Christian people against the threats of Islam and Buddhism."

"By nuking millions of African Christians?" Becky sarcastically remarked. "I think you're going to have to explain that one in some depth to the Lord when you meet him."

"Will that be soon?" Ava asked, with an alarming casualness.

"No. The Terran Union doesn't practice the death penalty. At least not officially. Some pirates have been known to fall out of an airlock from time to time..."

"So, life without parole then?"

"My guess is solitary confinement on somewhere like Calvados. I doubt they'd let you do hard labour on there, too many potential targets for your hate."

"Will I get a public trial?"

She wants to grandstand. That's why she surrendered. She loves making speeches and she'd have an interstellar audience. It would be the trial of the millennium.

Then an alarm rang.

And a computerised voice announced a chemical alert in the storage area.

Chapter 6

Grant Robinson was inventorying Ava Rice's clothing.

The garments were pretty much middle of the road in quality; apart from the uniform jacket and pants, which were custom-made, most the rest came from what appeared to be a company called American Apparel.

She looked over the boots.

"Two jackboots, size 40, black."

She passed over the footwear to Grant then moved to the belt.

"Hey, Sunita," Grant said, "there appears to be a catch here of some form..."

Sunita turned just in time to see him flick open the catch with his thumb... then get sprayed with something blue...

"Grant, what on... Grant!!!"

Grant fell to the floor and started convulsing rapidly, foaming at the mouth...

Sunita moved quickly to the communications console and stabbed the alarm button.

"Bridge, this is Storage! Lock down now, chemical!"

She heard the clunk of the vents shutting, the whirr of the hatches starting to shut as she turned back to Grant. Mouth to mouth was not advised for obvious reasons; all she could do was chest compressions.

The tune of the ancient nursery rhyme "Nelly the Elephant" came into her head from her first aid training, one of the six tunes with the correct rhythm for cardio-pulmonary resuscitation.

She pushed down, feeling the crack of broken ribs as she tried to keep her apprentice's heart going.

"Stay with me, Grant! Stay with me! Don't let Ava Rice claim another victim!"

The whole thing moved into a blur. For eight minutes, she continued to push until her husband arrived in an NBC suit.

"Sunita, he's gone," Daniel said sadly.

"Come on, Grant, stay with me! Don't die!"

"Sunny, he's gone! You've done all you can, but he's gone!"

****

The chemical alert alarm had wailed through the ship and Becky had swiftly moved to the intercom to ask what was going on. She did not get an answer.

"What have you done?!" Becky screamed at Ava Rice.

Ava smiled.

"I'm a National Socialist, remember? Don't you think that I'd have some form of cyanide pill on me?" she replied.

"Explain!" Becky demanded, now extremely concerned as to what had just happened to her friends.

"Well, not a pill. A spray hidden inside my boot. Open the heel in anything but a certain way and you get some lovely almond juice in the face."

The intercom went and Becky stabbed it quickly.

"Captain, what's going on here?"

"Grant Robinson's been exposed to cyanide. It doesn't look good."

"Understood. Rice put some in her boot as a suicide method."

Becky turned back to Ava, filling up with rage.

Lord Jesus, give me patience. Give me restraint. Because I'm considering breaking the Fifth Commandment.

"I'm a Christian. I try my dearest to be a good person. I am doing my utmost not to kill you *right now.*"

"I'm a Christian too. All my actions have been to protect God's people."

"That is the biggest load of bull... dung that I have ever heard in my life. You're going to have explain your actions to the Judge of All... and I severely doubt he's going to be overly impressed."

Becky delivered a hefty kick to one of the bars.

"Your actions put the survival of my *entire faith* in jeopardy! There are fourteen billion human beings now. Do you know many of them are Christians?"

"I get the feeling you're going to tell me."

"Two billion and that's the highest it has been for centuries! You're just one of a long line of hypocrites who have *completely ignored* the teachings of Jesus Christ! If I'm not worthy to untie the Lord's sandals, then you're not even worthy to be in the same city! I hope you *rot in hell!*"

Becky paused.

"You're not worth any more of my conversation, you, you, you - goat!"

Becky turned and sat down. It was not the world's greatest insult.

Now I know how the captors of other war criminals must have felt. A pity she didn't use the cyanide on herself.

She looked down at her shoulder holster, her hand moving towards opening it... then stopped.

Lord Jesus, give me patience, give me restraint...

She continued to watch her prisoner, wishing for Ava Rice to make some sudden attempt at escape so she could shoot her, then apologising to God for thinking that.

The communicator rang again.

"Becky, it's Alex. Grant's dead. Sunita did all she could."

"Thanks."

She prayed silently for the soul of the departed Grant Robinson. Not being one for gossip, she did not know about his relationship with Maria.

"How many people have you killed now?!" Becky screamed at Ava Rice.

"In the same room by my own hand? Nine," Ava replied.

"Nine?! Who were the other eight?"

Ava started counting them off.

"Four captured Liberty Republic scouts... three of their soldiers in a firefight... and one operator of a resistance forum in Boise. He doesn't really count though. I wasn't the one who pulled the lever... but I did make sure the rope was nice and long. Took his head nearly clean off."

Becky looked at Ava's face. She seemed pleased about this.

"You're a sadistic woman, aren't you?"

"Sadistic? Me? Not really? I wanted him dead quickly."

"It's not just nine, though, is it? It's all the other people you killed in your nuclear attack."

"No-one's actually given me the specific numbers for my part of the strike. Anyway, I thought you were done speaking with me."

"Shut up." Becky did not have anything else to say herself at this point.

Roughly 20 minutes later, the lights suddenly went off, being replaced with the red emergency lights.

"Guess some things haven't changed," Ava Rice remarked.

Becky reached for her communicator to report the fault.

Then there was a knock on the door of the brig. Becky got up and moved towards the entrance, opening it.

Standing outside was a figure holding something in its hand.

"Hi Maria, can I help you?"

Maria Penzance, her face a steely mask, hit her in the side of the head.

****

Sunita stood in the decontamination shower, her hands against the wall. She needed to spend 20 minutes in there to make sure all traces of the cyanide had gone from her skin.

She screamed an obscenity at the ceiling.

Grant Fletcher was dead. He had shown a lot of promise; a real keenness to learn and there was clearly a budding romance with Maria Penzance...

Now that was all over. Sunita had seen quite a few deaths in her time, she had even caused a couple herself, that cannibal on Desolation for example. But Grant was just a kid, barely nineteen.

I should go and kill Ava Rice right now. It's clear she just wants to grandstand in front of an interstellar audience. One shot and I'll be the woman who killed Rice.

She looked at the clock on the wall; two minutes left, then the drying sequence. Then she heard the gunshot.

"Weapons Discharge – Brig! Weapons Discharge – Brig!" came the automated alarm.

Guess someone had the same idea. Oh, f...

As soon as the booth was unlocked, Sunita put on a dressing gown and made her way to the brig.

Ava Rice was lying on the cell floor, blood pooling from her head. Becky Carrington was propped against the wall, looking shocked with blood running down her neck. Her weapon holster was unfastened. Her husband was looking at a medical scanner.

On the floor was a pistol and a black leather object.

And Maria Penzance was being physically restrained by Captain Widomski, screaming obscenities about Ava Rice.

"What happened!?" Sunita screamed.

Becky replied. She spoke even softer than usual, her eyes focussing on the more severely injured woman.

"Maria socked me with a sap... I managed to get up and grab her just as she fired."

Alexander spoke up.

"She's got brain function and a pulse. We need to get her to somewhere with better facilities ASAP. I'll call the doctor back."

Vanessa turned her head.

"Sunita. Find somewhere we can confine Maria that isn't a crime scene and get Marcus Larkov over here so we can take her there. Then get Marri to start prepping a jump for Zug Station as soon as humanly possible. We're going to have to perform a rapid deceleration at some point. Tell the Special Forces ship they're going to have to take over this operation... We're the fastest ship in this system and we need to get Rice some medical treatment."

****

Sunita returned to the bridge. Darius Marri turned and looked at her robe-clad form with a raised eyebrow.

"New uniform?" he asked.

"Shut it, Darius. Now is not the time." Sunita said to her superior officer. "Skipper needs an urgent jump for Zug Station plotted."

Marri turned to Forgan, in his pilot's chair.

"Forgan, maximum deceleration. Get us down to two hundred klicks per second."

He then hit the comm.

"Engineering, this is Bridge. We need to be ready for a jump..."

He looked down at his console and brought up the speed calculator. He added their current speed and the desired speed of two hundred kilometres per second. Then swore under his breath.

"... in about seven hours' time. Correction - make that eight. We need to get the shuttle back."

****

Back in the brig, Alex Carrington and ship's cook Daniel Bradshaw were placing Ava on a gurney to take her to the medical bay. Natalie Anvers, dressed in T-shirt and overall trousers, had arrived by this point, and was taking in the whole scene. Vanessa still had Maria in her grasp, with the latter starting to calm down.

As soon as Ava was taken from the scene, Natalie Anvers stopped looking down at the pool of blood on the floor, then looked Maria squarely in the eye. Her face showed abject fury.

"Sorry, what's your full name?" she asked.

"Maria Alison Landry Penz... What are you doing?"

"Maria Alison Landry Penzance, I am arresting you for attempted murder..."

Vanessa released Maria from her grip.

"Whoa, whoa. This is my ship - and Maria Penzance is in *my* custody. You are not arresting her. I already did that..." Vanessa replied before Natalie waved a hand to stop her.

"Well, I am. She committed an act of attempted murder. If Rice dies, second degree murder. Or more likely first since she clearly pre-meditated this."

"Against *Ava Rice*. Who has killed one of *my crew*. Who was Maria's boyfriend. Wish I could have learned that in happier circumstances. If it had not been so important to see this woman put on trial and I wasn't a New London Merchant Marine employee, I'd have airlocked her for that."

"What are you, a Spacee? No due process, just throw them into space..."

Vanessa slapped Natalie, who staggered back.

"Yes, I am actually. So are five other members of my crew. Four now. We deal with things in our own way... and we have due process. Unlike your Airlock Kickers..."

Natalie shook her head. She stopped for three long seconds.

"Sorry, I misspoke," she said.

"You *definitely* did."

"My point remains, though. I need Maria Penzance placed in my custody. Otherwise, you will be facing criminal charges for obstruction."

"You have *no* jurisdiction here. This is a New London flagged ship in interstellar space. That means New London law applies. If there is to be any criminal action, Maria is going before a jury there. I somehow doubt that the Crown Prosecution Service will file any charges in the circumstances, but I will detain Ms Penzance pending any instructions from my government."

"Check your Terran Union space law," Natalie replied. "I think you will find that Maria will need to be handed over to me or a Terran Union officer. That's the law."

Vanessa glared.

"I don't care about your law."

Maria spoke up.

"Can you please not talk about me like I'm not here? I'll happily defend my action in a court. No-one is going to convict me for this."

"I agree. Lieutenant Commander Anvers, go to your quarters and stay there. *Now.* The same applies for you, Ms Penzance."

****

"*Tulyar*, acknowledged. We'll be back at the shuttle in about five minutes," Hannah Wilmslow replied. "Doctor out."

"Right, let's close up the freezer and get out of here," Joaquin said. "This day is just getting worse and worse. I don't believe Maria Penzance could engage in attempted murder."

"I didn't think she'd be dating Grant. Now I've got to refresh myself on brain surgery," she said reaching to close up her medical bag.

"Brain surgery? You know how to do that?"

"The very basics, yes. Medical school covers the basics in pretty much everything and the specialist training on space medicine covers head injuries in more depth."

Hannah heard something trundling rapidly towards them and turned her head. A bulky maintenance robot came around the ring towards them.

"It should stop when it sees us," Joaquin said, as it then became obvious it would not... "Get clear!"

She was hauled up onto the top of the cryogenic chamber and then moved to pull the deputy engineer up. She got his feet clear just before the robot flew past them at 50 kilometres an hour, heading off on its route.

The two of them looked at each other.

"Wow, that was a close call..." Hannah said.

The two of them held each other for a second.

"I'd kiss you, but it's not appropriate, we're both wearing helmets and we have to perform brain surgery on a woman who committed genocide."

****

The two of them got out of the cryogenic wheel and started walking down the stairs that would take them back to the shuttle, where Otto Elven and Lyta Qarpik were waiting.

As they came down to the floor where *Walnut* was waking, Joaquin raised his own weapon.

"If Ava has been shot, these guys might do any..."

The two of them turned the corner into the docking bay... and found themselves face to face with a Nazi holding a machine pistol at them.

"Freeze!" the man yelled... as Joaquin aimed his own weapon at him.

Chapter 7

Hannah did not have her list of selected phrases immediately available. They were in her pocket and this was not the time to make any sudden moves in that direction. She raised her hands.

"Calm down," she said. "We need to make sure... Ava Rice shot. I doctor."

"Ava Rice shot. I know. You stay here." the goon said moving towards her, the weapon trained at her head.

Not best to lead on that, Hannah realised a bit too late.

"I save her. You let go. I save her," she continued. The man shook his head.

"No. Ava Rice come back here. You treat her on my ship."

Hannah was not exactly an expert on pidgin, but she could understand the situation. What she could not understand was how they knew that Ava Rice had been shot... perhaps they were listening in the comms.

"Better facilities on my ship. Let us go."

"Our leader was not guest. She was prisoner. You trick her."

They must have found a radio in the other shuttle... which would have all the standard civilian channels.

"If you kill me, she dies too."

She noticed Joaquin in her peripheral vision. He had his own weapon raised still, aiming at the goon's chest. She looked at his name tag. Moore.

"We only kill you if she dies. Call ship. Bring her here."

"Cannot do... every minute lower chance..."

"Die, you piece of...!" Joaquin suddenly cried. Hannah swung around to see Joaquin fire.

A three-round burst from his own submachine gun.

Then he pushed her to one side.

Six more rounds. Slamming into the chest of the Nazi.

Then silence.

The helmet reduced the sound of the shots from eardrum bursting down to merely very loud. She got to her feet than looked at Moore. His chest had multiple holes in, and he had taken a shot to the head.

He was beyond any help in this universe.

****

Hannah and Joaquin entered the shuttle. Lyta turned around, with her mouth open.

"There's blood on your..." Lyta said.

"Not mine. Some poor kid named Moore who Joaquin shot."

"I had to shoot him," Joaquin replied.

"I know," Hannah replied. "I don't like it, but I know. Tell *Tulyar* to switch channels, they're listening in."

She moved to her seat and started to strap in.

"I need the medical bay prepared for surgery," she instructed.

"Already being done," Lyta replied.

****

While they were decelerating, Joaquin Lugar was sitting with Captain Widomski and Clarissa Müller in her quarters, discussing the engineering aspects of *Horst Wessel*, nee *Rosa Parks*.

"I managed to grab some items of engineering interest from the ship and stashed them in the shuttle before the recall. Some of them might be of historical value," he said.

"That whole ship is of historical value," Müller added.

"Anyway, I found this... which I'm not entirely sure what it is..." Lugar pulled out a large sports bag from under the table.

"I was wondering what that was," Vanessa said. "I've seen your gym kit and it doesn't have that flag on it."

She saw a blue diagonal cross with white stars on it against a red background.

"I did some searching on topics related to the New Confederacy. This apparently was their military flag, with its roots going back to the 19th Century."

Joaquin reached into his pockets and put on some white cotton gloves.

"I don't want the oils in my fingers to damage some of the contents," he said.

"Good call. I had to do similar when I made some visits to the New London Royal Archives. Some of the official parchment there is over three hundred years old."

He opened the bag to pull out a large laptop computer, a bulky telephone of the sort used for ground to orbit communications and a bound notebook.

He placed the last of these on the table and gingerly opened it.

An array of numbers and letters on the table could be seen on the pages that were on display next to a group of names. There were various crossings out and alterations, but Vanessa Widomski's keen eye soon began to piece the things together. Her mouth dropped open.

"Joaquin, Clarissa. I think we have found the most consequential items in all of human history..."

Joaquin looked down.

"Abuja, Accra, Kumasi... those are all names of planets."

"Which were named after cities destroyed by Rice's nuclear strike. These were the notes she made for the targeting computer," Vanessa pointed at the laptop. "she used that and that satellite phone to fire forty-five missiles at West Africa and China. The Chinese fired back at the New Confederacy, which responded with their own missiles. Roughly eight hundred nuclear warheads – they never got an exact count – tore apart major cities of three nations and in Rice's case, ripped apart Chinese nuclear power stations to spread radiation over vast areas.

"The nuclear winter that followed, three years without a summer, saw 2.4 billion people die... and the survivors form the first government covering most of the human species. We're now onto the third, but we're no longer really fighting each other as a species anything as much as we used."

"We're fighting the Gan. In a cold war," Joaquin corrected.

"That is true... there's something awe-inspiring about this."

Clarissa spat on the floor.

"It's also horrific," she said. "Put it away. That is the bloodiest murder weapon in history."

Vanessa nodded.

"That's true. It'll probably end up in a museum as well."

****

Sitting in the Control Tower (the official term although it was more of a jutting out arm), Lieutenant Vincent Nguyen of the Terran Union Navy's Control Corps was monitoring the overall traffic picture when one of his Petty Officers raised her hand.

"Hyper pulse! Bearing One-Two-Eight, Positive Zero-Zero-Four! Range to follow."

Nguyen turned around and looked at the bright flash that had just appeared, visible from the windows of the Control Tower.

If we can see the flash from here... and it's at magnitude minus six or seven... then that's two to three light seconds out.

"Range is 1.5 light seconds. Transmission of identification coming through. Lima-Union-Foxtrot-Papa-Five-Five-Zero-One-Five. Fast Transport Ship *Tulyar...* issuing a Code Blue, sir!"

That's a medical emergency.

"Zug Station, this is *Tulyar*. We are requesting urgent docking clearance and medical assistance on docking. We have a patient with a gunshot wound on board. Copy, over," came the voice of Daniel O'Hanlon.

Nguyen indicated he was going to take the communication.

"*Tulyar*, this is Zug Station. We copy your last. We can get a trauma team ready for arrival at Docking Port... Four. Over," he replied.

Docking Port Four was the medical dock, used for major trauma cases or where the ship was containing infectious people.

"Roger. We will also need security escort for the patient. She is a wanted criminal at risk of potential harm. Over."

"Understood. Please transmit medical details and identification details. Over."

"Zug Station, please be advised that what is about to transmitted is No Drill and No Sike. Over."

No Sike? That's Spacee code for "I am not making this up."

"Go ahead, *Tulyar*. Over."

The medical data appeared on Nguyen's screen fifteen seconds later.

"Holy... *Tulyar*, please hold."

Nguyen picked up the telephone handset to call the Station Commander.

This is going to be the weirdest day of my life.

****

Hannah Wilmslow had found two members of the crew she trusted enough in this matter to move the gurney from the medical bay to the docking port: Alexander Carrington and his junior cargo hand Zhang De.

The final thrusts were being made to bring them to dock with Zug Station. A full trauma team was on standby to rush Ava Rice into surgery at the hands of an expert in the field.

The genocidal maniac was lying unconscious on the gurney below her. Hannah had removed part of Ava's skull - to her shock, she was using first name terms for this woman. to prevent dangerous swelling, inserted an endotracheal tube down her throat and given her anti-epilepsy medication to prevent seizures.

She mentally played the patient transfer information over for the medics...

****

Vincent Nguyen was standing by the docking port, waiting for the light to go green and for the four doors to open. A full trauma team had been assembled in the station's hospital and a route to it had been cleared, with uniformed soldiers at this military facility keeping people away. The lead doctor was standing by the airlock waiting to go, his Black Wilt assistant ready with a data pad.

The docking light went green and four metal doors rapidly pulled open.

A red-haired middle-aged woman strode quickly forward, followed by two humans bearing a gurney that they got over the threshold. The woman moved immediately to get the wheels down. Then she began speaking loudly and quickly, but still made sure to enunciate.

"Ava Rice, apparent biological age 35, Terran female. Single .22 gunshot wound to the head, ten hours ago. Medical history completely unavailable..."

****

Vanessa Widomski walked into her personal bathroom and flipped open the panel to run herself an herbal bath. She needed something to reduce her stress level. Especially after today.

What had started off as the opportunity of a lifetime was now a nightmare. She had a dead crew member in her freezer, his remains awaiting a post-mortem and then a space burial. The person who would conduct that was currently working on keeping Ava Rice alive.

She had heard nothing about that from Dr Wilmslow. She would not until the outcome was clear, one way or the other.

She removed her jacket and flung it to her side. She was pulling her shoes off when the intercom rang. She moved over to it and pressed the audio button to pick up the call. She did not recognise the number. Probably a public terminal.

"Widomski speaking," she replied.

"Hey, Captain, it's Louisa Landry. Just seen the doctor at the clinic," replied her gunner. She sounded calm.

"How was it?"

"My vision's coming back already. No permanent damage it seems."

"That's good. I've already lost one crew member today. Make that two. I need to prepare the termination papers for Maria," Vanessa noted.

"You're firing her?" Landry asked.

"No choice really. Hitting Becky like that meant was a sackable offence before she decided to shoot Ava Rice."

"You know, that's going to put her in the history books."

"That's not something that I am really concerned about at present."

"Understood, ma'am. Landry out."

Vanessa was about to remove her other clothing when there was a sharp knocking on the door to the corridor.

Who in Io is that? Vanessa thought. *I gave instructions that I was not to be disturbed...*

She walked quickly towards the door and opened it.

Darius Marri was standing in front of her, with Natalie Anvers standing slightly behind him.

"What is it?" she barked.

"Sorry, Captain, but I needed to run this by you urgently," he said.

"Well, I was about to have a bath. Can it wait until after that?"

"Not really," Natalie said.

"I thought I told you to stay in your quarters."

"Well, I need your security footage and access to the brig to take photographs of the crime scene." Natalie was looking like she would not take no for an answer, but also sad about the situation.

"Why?"

"For the criminal investigation."

"This is out of your jurisdiction. Interstellar Space starts at one hundred Astronomical Units from system barycentre. We were closer to five hundred when Rice was shot."

"Look up the Terran Union Criminal Code. Section 5. Our jurisdiction extends to five hundred."

"Mr Marri, please check this while I have my bath."

"Already have, ma'am," Marri said. "Sadly, she's right."

"So," Natalie continued, "you can give it to me now or once I report in, the gendarmes will turn up with a warrant."

Vanessa sighed.

"Mr Marri, please give this creature what it wants."

****

Two hours later. Major Katrin Tamm, Station Commander of Zug Station, was sitting in her office, drafting a message for Helvetios Command on Basel to inform them of the situation.

Station Commander of an outer system station meant wearing multiple hats. Mayor, Sheriff, Treasurer and on occasion, actual military leader.

But nothing in her training had prepared her for the situation she was undergoing today. Especially as the first thing that she had heard about Ava Rice being on *Rosa Parks* was Lieutenant Nguyen's call. The daily dispatch boat was due in another six hours and that would hopefully have some instructions as to she was supposed to do.

Her intercom rang and she stabbed the button.

"I've got a Lieutenant Commander Anvers here to see you, sir," came the voice of the young private who served as her personal assistant.

"Send her through."

The door opened, to reveal a blonde-haired woman wearing a T-shirt with the legend 'I DON'T CARE'. She had a satchel on her shoulder.

Anvers snapped to attention and placed her hand on her heart in the non-covered salute.

"Lieutenant Commander Anvers, TUSS *Emilia Plater*, reporting, sir."

Tamm rolled her eyes, then went formal.

"Where is your uniform? And why are you not on your ship?" she asked.

"My uniform was on my ship, which was wrecked by fire from our hijacked shuttle."

"Start from the beginning, please. That's an order."

Anvers related the story of what had happened, with Tamm asking probing questions.

"I have the security footage here and a camera with photographs of the crime scene. I wish to add a personal recommendation to the end of this report," she concluded.

"Go ahead."

"No charges against Maria Penzance."

Tamm looked down a minute. Her mind running through the options.

"No. I am referring this to the prosecutor for a charge of attempted murder, along with actual body harm against this Rebecca Carrington," she said, very firmly.

"In the circumstances, I do not think that is wise."

"Explain please."

"This is Ava Rice we are talking about. A genocide-committing maniac. Do you honestly think the cause of justice is served by charging Maria Penzance?"

"Personally, yes. But I would be failing in my legal and moral duty if I let this slide. Even for Ava Rice."

"I thought that too, but I realised the extremities of the circumstances. I wish my objections to be formally recorded."

"They shall be. Now go find yourself a proper uniform."

****

Vanessa had her bath and then started the process of writing a dispatch for her bosses in New London. Checking the schedule for the dispatch boat on the station's network, she figured that it would take about 15 hours for her message to arrive at the Helvetios Beacon to join the queue for forwarding. The Beacon network out to the Hyades Cluster generally had a transmission time of six hours to reach New London.

So basically, she would have to wait for two days for any reply. She fired up the computer on her desk to bring up her message writing software, read an email, then she wrote her report.

Maria shot Ava Rice. That's going to put her in the history books. I'm probably going to be in the history books.

As she did, she looked at the Terran Union Criminal Code. This confirmed that Natalie Anvers had told her. She saw a note that the Commonwealth of New London did not recognise this claim, but she severely doubted they would be able to do anything about except for raise a diplomatic protest. She added this to the report.

The on-board databanks also contained the Terran Union's sentencing guidelines. She selected the 'Colony Systems' rules, which covered the unincorporated territories like Helvetios.

She looked through the guidelines. She had a good knowledge of civil law as she was a qualified notary public, which allowed her to conduct weddings. She was not an expert on criminal law, but she knew enough to realise that Maria was in deep trouble.

She completed her report. It was a short affair of about five hundred words. She then started the process of converting the report into the telegraphic code to reduce its length and enciphering the message using the New London Merchant Navy's Ten-Riddle system. Once it was done in ten minutes' time, she would contact Stellar Union and get it sent.

Now it was time to do something hard but necessary. She opened the intercom and rang Maria's room.

"Ms Penzance, please come to my office."

Maria acknowledged this and Vanessa hung up. She reached for her cap and stood ready.

Three minutes passed. There was a knock on the door.

"Come in," Vanessa instructed. Maria walked in. She had something in her hands.

"Thought I'd save time on this," Maria said, then placed the items on the desk in front of them.

Vanessa looked down. Maria's rank insignia, her Tulyar patches, her corporate identity card, and her key to the liquor cabinet.

"Thinking ahead. Shame you didn't do that before storming into a cell and shooting an unarmed prisoner," Vanessa began, sounding more sad than angry. No-one liked to see her angry, even her late husband.

"That prisoner murdered my boyfriend," Maria replied.

"I know, I know... but I wish you hadn't done that. I'm losing a good crew member as a result. Do you have any regrets?"

"Not personally. I think I did humanity a favour by shooting that woman. Well, an excuse for a woman."

"Well, you of course understand I have to terminate you for this. With prejudice."

“Of course.”

“And for assaulting Becky Carrington,” Vanessa added.

“Now that I do regret. I figured that she was too good to let me shoot Rice.”

“I’ll tell her you said that. She’s also told me that she doesn’t wish to press charges against you.”

“That’s appreciated. Please pass on my apologies to her.”

“I’m going to allow you to stay on the ship, confined to quarters, until the Terran Union authorities decide what to do about criminal charges.”

“Thank you.”

“I’m not a lawyer, and I suggest you get a good one, but you’re not likely to be in a good position should they decide to charge you.”

“I figured that.”

“If you’d been prosecuted in New London, you’d have a decent chance of convincing a jury to find you not guilty.”

“That was what I was hoping,” Maria observed with a wry smile.

“But this is the Terran Union. They have five judges to decide your guilt or innocence. Unless you manage to bribe two of them, then they will decide based on the law and the facts. Not their emotions.”

“Which I figure won’t be good for me.”

"You're likely to be convicted for attempted murder. The starting point for that is 17 years in prison, of which you would have to serve at least eleven."

"That's if Ava Rice lives."

"Quite... and if she dies, you're looking at a life sentence with 30 years minimum."

****

Sunita Kumar, as Security Officer, was sitting outside *Tulyar*'s starboard docking port in Docking Corridor 4 of Zug Station. Her job was to log members of the crew going into and out of the ship, to make sure that everyone was accounted for.

Naturally, the situation with Marie was on her mind. It was going to be on everyone's for months. Sooner or later, the Terran Union were going to show up with a warrant...

She heard the clumping of heavy boots down the corridor and got to her feet.

Does Zug Station have a Procurator? Sunita wondered. She did not need to wonder for long.

A group of eight assault rifle bearing black uniformed soldiers wearing armoured vests saying GENDARMERIE were walking towards her, flanking two other uniformed people.

One of them was Natalie Anvers, wearing a full naval dress uniform that was slightly too big for her. Her face was a mask. The other was a heavy-set man in his thirties with dark brown skin and dressed in grey uniform with white piping. He was holding a scroll in his hand.

Sunita's hand started to move instinctively to her holster, but she checked it in time as a couple of rifles were raised in her direction. She raised her own hands.

These people will shoot me if I do anything stupid.

The grey uniformed man came up to her. His name badge read BOWLER and he spoke with a distinctive accent that Sunita could not quite place.

"Are you Captain Vanessa Widomski?" he asked.

"No, I'm Warrant Officer Sunita Kumar. As my badge indicates."

The man unrolled the scroll.

"Noted. I am Captain Henry Bowler of the Terran Union Military Procurator Service. I am the designated prosecutor for Zug Station in all criminal matters and have been assigned Case 290/HEL/2619, namely the attempted murder of Ava Jessica Rice on 18 August 2619."

Sunita rolled her eyes.

"Do we *have* to do this whole rigmarole?"

"Yes, we do. I have probable cause to believe that the suspect, Maria Alison Landry Penzance, is located upon the vessel known as FTS *Tulyar* and that the scene of the crime is located upon the same vessel.

Accordingly, with the concordance of Justice Thurgood Dred Scott, I hereby issue this warrant..."

It went on for two minutes. Basically, he had a warrant to board the ship, obtain forensic evidence and arrest Maria Penzance.

"Can I at least inform Ms Penzance that you're coming in, so she surrenders herself peacefully?"

"You can do that."

"Also, can we avoid cuffing her? She's been through enough already."

"That is not an option."

"Well, you're... unpleasant." Sunita said, deciding that swearing at this guy was not going to help matters.

Sunita moved to the communication console and tapped the button to call the Captain.

"Captain, this is Front Porch. We've got some gendarmes here to arrest Maria Penzance and search the ship."

"Right, let's do this," Vanessa replied.

****

Maria put up no resistance as she was handcuffed and led off the ship. The other officers were conducting a search and Sunita heard a call to get a forensic team over to collect samples from the brig.

As Sunita was sitting at the entrance, Dr Anvers came up to her.

"Sunita..." she said. Sunita turned slowly and barked a response.

"Clear off, Lieutenant Commander Anvers."

"I suspect you don't like me very much at the moment..."

"That's an understatement."

"Can you please hear me out for a second?"

"Why? You're just going to give some warped justification for your actions."

"I'm not. My report explained the full circumstances behind what had happened. I've personally recommended *no* criminal charges against Miss Penzance."

"That's nice," Sunita sneered.

"I snapped at all of you. I'm sorry. However, the matter was taken out of my hands as soon as we docked at this station. It would have been anyway. There are people who will want to throw the book at Miss Penzance for the embarrassment she's caused. They'll have lost the case of their careers, Bowler in particular. He's a toady, as I discovered today."

"Not a surprise. The way he read that warrant to me."

"My uncle won't be happy either. He's Chief Prosecutor for Terra."

"Who would have handled the case against Rice, I imagine," Sunita remarked.

"If I hadn't followed procedure, I would have been prosecuted too."

"There we go..." Sunita remarked. "Thinking of yourself."

"It would have made no difference to Maria's fate. Anyway, I'm going to get you a really good lawyer... and I'm going to pay for it myself."

Sunita paused as she ran that through her mind.

"Wow, I... that makes up for it. Slightly. Still, get out of my sight before Bowler has to add an assault charge to his docket."

Sunita Kumar watched as Anvers turned on her heels and walked off, her head slumped. She felt slightly sorry for her, but only a little. Sunita's own head slumped and she thought about the twists of fate that brought them here. The reward they were getting was going to be big, but it felt dirty now that she had lost one friend to murder and another was now going to prison.

She herself then turned back towards the ship.

"Sunita!" came a cry from behind her. The Security Officer turned back, seeing Doctor Wilmslow only six metres away from her. She jumped slightly.

"Sorry, I didn't notice you..."

"I did call you. Twice." Hannah said. Sunita realised that if the doctor had wanted to kill her, that lapse of attention could have been the last one she had had in this world. The doctor's face was a mask.

"What happened?"

"85% of people who are shot in the head die, either instantly or within a few hours. Ava Rice... is one of the 15% who are going to live."

Chapter 8

President Said-Alvarez was looking out of the window of *Luna One*, the dedicated surface to orbit transport for his ship, at the Neil Armstrong Casino Resort, part of the Tranquillity Base city/tourist trap. He was waiting here for the security sweep to be done for his trip to the government compound over at Surveyor 5 Town, twenty-five kilometres to the north-northeast, where he was going to be having a lot of meetings.

There then came a knock at the door, which was opened by one of his Secret Service guards.

"Jessica Chan to see you, Mr President."

Said-Alvarez sighed. Chan was one of the press corps... and one of the more annoying ones. From the tabloid newspaper *Human Interest*, she had published some of the more lurid details of his junior wife's infidelity with his former Treasury Secretary. If he had been a dictator, he would have put her in jail.

Yet as a democrat, I must give her press access because the fact I don't like her isn't a valid reason to revoke her pass.

Chan opened the door, her white curls bouncing with excitement. The President turned around slowly supporting his slightly overweight form on an ornate cane to look at her.

"Mr President," she began, "do you have any comment on reports that Ava Rice is in hospital on Zug Station, Helvetios, having been shot in the head?"

* * * *

Justice Thurgood Dred Scott looked at the prisoner in front of him, the photographs below him and then the two lawyers flanking the former. Procurator Henry Bowler and Counsellor Laura Stewart were well known to him, as the best lawyers on the station.

They were the only lawyers on the station.

In any event, this was all a far cry from the usual bar fights and fee disputes that he had to adjudicate on in this one-reactor town. The small courtroom, currently cleared of everyone bar himself, the lawyers, the prisoner and one Gendarme, was in no way set up for a major trial. That would have to be done on Basel.

"Does the accused have anything to say in this matter?" he asked.

"No comment," came the reply from Maria Penzance.

Probably wise at this stage, Judge Dred Scott thought.

Scott reached for his digital scanner and added his thumb print to the charge sheet.

"Your charge is accepted and approved, Procurator Bowler. I want to move to the question of bail. Counsellor Stewart, do you wish to request bail?"

"Yes, I do. My client has no previous record and has told me that she has every intention of standing trial to make her case," Stewart said in a matter-of-fact manner with no emotion either way.

Bowler huffed.

"I object," he replied. "She is a clear flight risk. She has no ties to Helvetios and is the crew member of a fast freight..."

"She was fired from that post." Stewart's tone grew more strident.

"Let the Procurator say his piece, then you can respond." Scott raised his hand.

"Fast freighter. Furthermore, given her clear animus towards Ava... I cannot believe I am saying this..."

"We all can't - but continue."

"... Ava Rice, there is reason to believe she may make a further attempt on that woman's life."

Maria was about to say something and then was silenced by what Scott thought was a quick kick in the shin. Scott knew that Stewart commonly did this to quiet defendants who were in danger of self-incriminating and the smile at the end was her tell.

"Captain of Justice Bowler, the craziness of this situation has clearly gotten to your head. Look at this young woman. She was prevented from actually killing Ava, let's not use her name shall we... her target because she was wrestled to the ground by an Offred from Dom Pennsylvania she'd failed to adequately knock out."

Maria opened her mouth and then cried in pain.

"Sorry, my foot slipped. She is hardly likely to be able to get past four gendarmes and several hospital staff."

Scott nodded and thought for a few seconds.

"Agreed. Bail set at 10,000 credits. Accused is not to leave Zug Station, is not to enter the hospital facility without prior approval and an escort and is prohibited from speaking to the media directly. Also, I am giving the defendant the standard anonymity in cases like this; the newspapers will refer to her as Maria P. I have ruled."

He grabbed his gavel... and then the head broke off as he struck it.

* * * *

Major Ortega was starting to suit up ahead of the boarding operation, donning her dark grey combat armour with bulletproof shielding around the helmet and oxygen tanks. Her officer's pistol was on the table in front of her, along with her cutlass.

Spacecraft were often confined environments where shooting weapons was not always advised. Sometimes you needed to get hand to hand and as a result an old weapon had made a comeback in some circles; they were also useful for cutting through cables and other obstacles.

The helmet had a narrow vision slit with a tactical display that was projected in front of the user's eyes. She put this on and looked out of the window at their quarry, just sixty kilometres away. It was marked as Tango One.

Whether they're going to put up a fight remains to be seen. If they start a fight, I will certainly end it – and win it.

Suddenly, an object detached itself from Tango One. It swiftly gained the appellation Tango Two.

"Captain, Combat Information. It looks like some form of shuttle has detached itself from Tango One," came a call over her helmet radio.

Is that an attack run?

"Go to Red Alert." Ortega ordered.

You want a piece of me? Well, you're going to end up like Hitler... Er, what did happen to Hitler? I'll have to check.

Then the hull of *Rosa Parks* was marked with a series of silent flashes and fireballs. The ship broke into several large pieces, along with many smaller bits of debris...

“Captain, Tango One has blown itself up!”

“I can see that Combat. I’m looking at it.”

I think Hitler shot himself to avoid capture. Well, this has turned into something completely different. I was so looking forward to shooting some live targets too.

“Captain to All Stations. Retrieve Tango Two, assuming it doesn’t try to shoot us. We’d better get a team to have a look through the wreckage.”

Chapter 9

It had been a day since the shooting.

The dispatch boat that came out from the Helvetios Beacon to the five outlying stations brought not only military and government traffic but also civilian messages, fast freight, and paper post. The offices of Stellar Union, the major BeaconGram company, were the primary place for the non-military population to receive and send messages, with their attached café being a good place to catch up on the gossip.

Sunita Kumar had decided to retire to a café after visiting the funeral director to arrange Grant's wake, which would occur tomorrow. Spacee funerals tended to be done as quickly as possible with at least two wakes, sometimes three. Then there was the Wake of Wakes for all the departed on All Souls' Day that occurred every 2 November.

This was followed by Sore Heads Day, a national holiday in several polities.

As she ordered at the counter, dressed in her formal *Tulyar* uniform, she noticed a man in a fedora with the word 'PRESS' on a card in the hat band.

Sunita swore under her breath as she moved to an empty table and sat down. It was probably only a matter of time before this got out.

"Who are you?" she asked as the man pulled out a notepad from his pocket.

"Warren Wiltshire, *Helvetios Daily.* Would you like to answer some questions about the extraordinary story you're in the middle of?" he asked with a pronounced drawl that one associated with the Pegasus-Pisces sector. He looked young and keen.

"*Helvetios Daily?*" Sunita asked. "What goes on in this system that warrants a daily news programme?"

"To be honest, mostly bar fights and bake sales," Wiltshire replied. "This is the biggest story I've had in my life and I'd like an exclusive. We're a small independent channel, not a big corporation's branch."

"I've been told to refer any media approaches to my Captain."

"You can't give me any off the record comments?"

The reporter's insistence was starting to annoy Sunita, a woman of short temper at the best of times.

"Nothing printable. I'll take your card and give it to my Captain... and if you bother me again, you will be singing soprano."

At that point, the man behind the counter called out.

"News is on!"

The dispatch boat had obviously sent over the news broadcasts from Helvetios to be played over the station's internal network.

The station ident of TDK One appeared with a countdown to programme start. When it hit zero, a heavily made-up Mongolian woman appeared in the studio standing next to a holographic image of Ava Rice.

"The ultimate blast from the past has turned up in Helvetios. Ava Rice, who committed genocide over five centuries ago, is alive and in critical condition in hospital."

They spent fifteen minutes of a thirty-minute programme covering the news, using a lot of words to say little. The pertinent discussion was how Ava Rice had managed to escape from Terra and end up all the way in the Helvetios system in the first place. They had put in a request for more information from Terra on *Rosa Parks*. Sunita wondered herself... then recalled the data she had seen on the Arecibo message.

She must have planned her escape, Sunita realised. *Why else would she have the targeting computer on the ship in the first place? Because she launched the ground-based missiles while in orbit.*

Sunita imagined the string of flashes that Rice would have seen from *Rosa Parks* as the missiles she had launched hit home.

She faked her death. Ultimately a coward, she didn't care about anyone else... and removed herself from the situation so she didn't have to see the consequences of her actions.

Warren spoke up.

"I suspect that you're going to get a lot more approaches. At least from the Big Seven and likely others."

"The Big Seven?" Sunita asked.

"The main media companies," Warren replied, reeling off a list of names that Sunita mostly recognised. "They'll dramatically sensationalise the whole affair. We won't."

"I will bear that in mind..."

Sunita took the card. Someone on another table came over to her. He was a young man from a mining ship, wearing some very grubby overalls.

"Hey, are you from *Tulyar*? The ship that captured Ava Rice," he asked.

"Yes..." Sunita replied, wary of where this was going.

"I'd like to have a nightcap with you."

Sunita could have said something witty, but instead was just direct.

"Go away, silicon breath. I'll have that bagel and coffee to go!"

****

"Zug Station, Zug Station, this is Mail Ship *Patrick Greendale*, requesting permission to dock."

Vincent Nguyen looked at the clock on the wall. Forty minutes late.

"*Patrick Greendale*, this is Zug Station. You're a bit later than usual," he replied.

"We got a last-minute call for three passengers on board. First one's Johanna Orlov-Park."

Vincent scanned his memory.

Best criminal defence lawyer in the subsector. This is going to be fun.

"Noted. What about the others?"

The visitors would need to be added to the log in case of emergencies.

"Piers Solomon and Hans Werner."

Vincent recognised the former name.

"A TV journalist?"

"And his producer."

"Right, I guess they're all here in connection with the Tulyar situation. I was about to call them up anyway."

Vincent started the process of making the call.

****

The daily officers' meeting on Tulyar was not usually daily but was at the moment. In this case, the five human beings that made up the officers of Tulyar were in Vanessa's quarters.

Clarissa poured out a bottle of Miner's Mead that she had bought on the station for four of them, including herself.

Darius Marri stuck with orange juice.

"So, Captain," he began. "Any news back from New London?"

"Well," Vanessa replied with a straight face, "we had a message approving our involvement in the whole *Rosa Parks* operation and congratulating us on having a front row seat in history."

"I would love to have been a fly on Sir Eleanor's wall when she heard your report."

"Indeed. She has also given me full latitude on selling our story to the press."

She saw the look on Darius' face.

"Yes, I'm surprised you didn't realise that. We'd have gotten a fair bit of media interest anyway just for finding a Generation Ship. Finding a Generation Ship with Ava Rice in is like..."

"Two royal flushes in a row?" Sunita asked.

"Not the metaphor I would have used," Vanessa replied. "More like their birthday, anniversary and religious holiday of choice had all come at once."

"I had an approach from a journalist myself."

"Oh really, Mrs Kumar? Why didn't you tell me earlier?"

"Saw me in the café after I arranged the funeral... I was going to save it for this meeting."

"Acceptable, barely," Vanessa looked sour... then smiled. "I've had two approaches myself via BeaconGram. LiveFeed Channel 4 and Sun Times A-Star want to interview me as well as other members of the crew. Suspect we will be getting more approaches. Who spoke to you?"

"Someone from *Helvetios Daily*. Believe they're from an independent channel."

"Well, once we get them all in, I will evaluate them and make a decision. I don't know about you, but I am inclined to go for the independent so they can sell it on to other networks.

"We could always start a bidding war, drive up the price," Sunita suggested.

"Let's not act like prostitutes, Mrs Kumar."

"Apologies ma'am."

"Anyway, we need to get a new main gun from somewhere. Our one is completely wrecked. The NLMN's insurance policies will ultimately cover the loss."

"Yes, Sunita added. "but 'we will send you a cheque in four or five months' doesn't tend to go well with most repair companies, I tend to find.

"There are two repair facilities here. One of them is military and the other one only sells mining equipment. I'm not optimistic about 51 Peg either. I've got someone coming to fix the hull damage and remove the old gun for scrap."

The intercom rang at this point. Vanessa got up and moved to pick up the call.

"Go ahead, Mr O'Hanlon."

The communications officer smiled at her.

"Got a Lieutenant Nguyen on the line for you. Wants to make you an offer you can't refuse."

"Go ahead," Vanessa replied, wondering what this was.

The visage of Vincent Nguyen appeared on the screen.

"Hello, Captain Widomski. I understand that you've got a wrecked cannon on your ship."

"That would be correct," Vanessa replied.

"Would you like a replacement?"

"Yes, I would."

"For free?"

"Lieutenant, you are testing my pat... for free?"

"That is correct."

"You have a spare cannon just lying around? Did it fall off the back of a transport?"

"No, it's not stolen, if that's what you mean."

Vanessa realised that humanity was a single species divided by many languages... sometimes the same one.

"I meant, is it a junkyard salvage?"

"No, not all. Genuine brand-new weapon, given to you free of charge as a gesture of our appreciation."

"Noted," Vanessa replied, also realising getting a new weapon now would mean they were away from this station a lot quicker.

"Brand new Coyote Perlman 340. We had one just come in. Two six-barrels, three hundred rounds of 502-millimetre, lead computer, automatic loading."

"I am not a gun expert, so I will get back to you on that."

She pressed the mute button.

"Take it," Darius said. "It's one of the best on the civilian market."

Vanessa looked around for comments from the others.

"It will increase our power draw on the reactor, but nothing we can't handle," Clarissa added.

"I'm the doctor. If it means I don't have to do emergency surgery, so be it," Hannah replied.

"A lead computer system is something we would definitely need; we were very lucky to be firing on a stationary target," Sunita concluded. "But make sure it actually works before we leave the system."

Vanessa moved over and unmuted the call.

"We'll take it."

Vincent's mouth moved but no sound came out.

"Lieutenant..." Vanessa saw a classic icon on the screen. "You're on mute."

Vincent turned his sound back.

"Excellent. I will get the installation arranged. Also, we've got three visitors for you. Well, one of them is probably for Maria Penzance."

"Go ahead."

"A journalist and his camera guy, along with a criminal defence lawyer from Helvetios."

"That last one is definitely for Maria Penzance then. I'll let her know she's coming."

"Thank you, *Tulyar*. I will let you know if there is anything else. Out."

The call disconnected.

"Well," Sunita said. "Tie me up and call me Lucy. That Anvers came through."

****

An hour later, Maria Penzance was sitting in her room in the Zug Station Hotel, watching a comedy that she was not exactly enjoying when the intercom rang. Reception had been told to screen any visitors for her.

She picked up the handset.

"Ms Penzance?" the receptionist began. "There are two lawyers here to see you. Names of Laura Stewart and Johanna Orlov-Park."

"Right," Maria gulped. "Send them up."

Maria did some quick tidying of her room and straightened her hair before there was a knock on the door.

She opened the door to reveal the blonde middle-aged curls of Laura Stewart and another woman. The latter was a tall and striking woman with pinkish skin and East Asian facial features.

Laura was dressed in a pretty average grey suit and white blouse, but her partner was attired much more extravagantly.

Johanna Orlov-Park wore an expensive black suit with a near ankle-length skirt, buckle shoes and a white blouse done up to her neck with a bolo tie incorporating a diamond clip with no less than four carats worth of diamonds. Maria's mother had been a jeweller, so Maria knew a bit about gems.

"You must be Maria Penzance," Orlov-Park said with a distinctive drawl. "My name is Counsellor Johanna Orlov-Park. I've been hired to represent you in your upcoming criminal matter."

"Yes, I'm Maria," Maria replied, then realised that answer was not the best response.

"Sit down on the bed. I've had a brief discussion with Advocate Stewart here and I think I've got a good idea of what has happened."

Laura handed over a suitcase. Orlov-Park opened it to display a holographic projector, which she turned on.

A display appeared on the projector with the words 'Murder under Terran Law'.

"Oh, yes, I have some papers for you to sign. We'll do them after this if you agree to be represented by me," the Counsellor continued.

"Got it."

"Now, you have been charged under Section 20/5 of the Terran Union Colony Systems Criminal Code, for the attempt to murder Ava Rice. The facts of the case as I see them are such. After she killed your boyfriend via a booby-trapped shoe, you decided after about thirteen minutes to take a sap from your room and go to the brig, where you arrived fifteen minutes after that and struck Rebecca Carrington across the head and then took her firearm. After a delay of about two minutes, during which you let out some pretty strong statements towards Ava Rice that I won't repeat here, you fired the weapon just as Rebecca Carrington rugby tackled you."

"That's correct with one error," Maria said. "I didn't actually know that Grant was dead at the time, but I strongly believed it to be the case. Rice pretty much agreed he was dead when I confronted her from what I could understand of her old English."

Orlov-Park tapped the display, bringing up 'Attempted Murder'.

"Indeed, I think there is no question of your guilt in this matter. Now, it looks likely that Ava Rice is going to live, otherwise you'd be looking at mitigated murder. That's certainly what I would be arguing for."

She took Maria through the elements of the offence by virtue of a presentation, the display altering as she went through each point. Maria felt a slight pang of guilt as it slowly become clear to her that she was bang to rights on this. Only a sympathetic jury would acquit her and the Terran Union did not use juries.

"I think we can argue that you were clearly provoked to rage by the murder of Grant Robinson. However, the prosecution will argue that your actions were pre-meditated due to the fact that you waited a considerable time and planned the offence, namely by grabbing the sap. Over half an hour wait according to the log."

"Yes, and I'm not entirely sure I regret it," Maria replied.

"That's something I would strongly advise you *not* to say in court," Johanna said.

"What if they ask me under oath? I'm not going to lie."

"You exercise your right to silence. A bit better than you did in the bail hearing by all accounts."

Maria huffed and glared at Laura.

"Snitch," she said.

Laura rolled her eyes. Johanna gave Maria another disapproving look.

"Now, there will be five judges in your hearing, which will be on Basel. Four of them are needed for a conviction. The Prosecutor, probably Louis Galveston, will outline the charges, then you will have a chance to plead guilty or not guilty. If you plead not guilty, both of us will make an initial speech, then the judges will ask witnesses and receive evidence. Both of us can also ask questions. Then there will be closing speeches and a chance for you to say something before they retire to consider their verdict. They will come back and in the high probability they convict you, your sentence will generally be issued there and then. Got that?"

"Could they find me not guilty?"

"Unlikely. That's why I am suggesting a plea bargain. You're looking at ten years at a guess. I may be able to get that down to four or five."

"Four or five years?" Maria replied, in shock.

"Yes, that's right. You did go into a cell, hit someone round the head, steal their gun and shoot a defenceless prisoner in the head. Unless I can pull off a miracle, the question is how long you get and what kind of prison you end in. Now, let's get the representation agreement signed, because you're not going to get any better lawyer around here."

****

The wreckage of *Rosa Parks* was slowly spreading out. Cryogenic pods hang in deep space, their inhabitants dead inside after the temperature controls lost power, floating with other frozen corpses. Paperwork, personal effects, and farming equipment accompanied them.

The Special Forces dressed in their grey armoured space suits and McCandless Chairs, the untethered mobility units used for boarding operations, were going through the wreckage, retrieving anything of historical interest.

Margaret Carter had been instructed to stay alongside the wreckage until it swept its way out of the system; in four days' time, it would reach its closest distance of about four Astronomical Units from Helvetios but was travelling far too quickly to be captured by the system's gravity, so would travel relatively quickly back out into deep space.

It was unlikely that they were going to get any lookie-loos or looters, but you never knew.

****

Dora Ortega looked at the seven men and one woman in her holding cell.

She scratched her head, wondering how precisely she was going to communicate with these people. They understood simple instructions, like "Hands up," but she was going to need to find a qualified linguist or...

She had an idea. She moved towards her radio.

"Carter Six to Four-Zero-Two. Come down to the holding cell please," she instructed.

She walked over to the table and opened a can of Tango that she had picked up from the Navy Exchange kiosk on her ship, home to 114 Special Forces personnel. She opened it and took a swig.

The eight prisoners looked sullen and resigned. Unwilling for whatever reason to kill themselves, they had decided to surrender themselves to the Terran Union.

"Tango?" one of them called.

She pulled the can down and looked at the man. He was about the same age as her in his late thirties, dressed in a black combat uniform of an incredibly old style with lightning bolts on the collars and a red, white, and blue flag on the left arm. The name on his jacket said "DONALDSON".

"Donaldson? You know Tango?" she growled.

"Favourite drink. Happy it survived," Donaldson said in halting Manglish.

'Four-Zero-Two,' also known as Sergeant Peter Kinoster, arrived at this point.

"You wanted to see me, sir," he said. She reached for a disposable face mask and handed it to him. They were to wear them whenever they were within two metres of the prisoners to avoid the risk of infecting them with some disease that the 21ˢᵗ century arrivals had yet not encountered.

"Yes, you speak German, don't you?" she asked.

"That is correct."

"How much has it changed over the centuries?"

"Not that much."

"See if any of these lot understand German."

"Sorry, sir?" Kinoster looked very confused.

"They're Nazis. I seem to recall that the lead Nazi was a German."

"No, he wasn't."

"I'm sorry. Are you contradicting me?"

"He was Austrian. Didn't become a German citizen until 1932."

"Whatever. Talk to these people."

Kinoster walked as close as he dared to the bars of the cell, then barked something in German. All of the prisoners inside stood to attention.

Dora Ortega grinned. This was working now.

"Tell them that I want to speak to whoever is in charge."

Kinoster did so. A few seconds later, another man in his late thirties stepped forward. Ortega was not an expert on New Confederacy rank insignia, but he appeared to be an officer.

"Bring him to my office."

****

The three of them ended in Ortega's office, sat three metres apart with Kinoster acting as a translator.

"So, I guess I'm the first person that you've spoken to in this particular new world you find yourself in," she began.

"Yes, that is correct. Permit me to introduce myself, ma'am. My name is Captain Peter Sumpter of the New Confederacy Security Division."

"My name is Major Dora Ortega of the Terran Union Special Forces and your government hasn't existed since 2099, when your commander started a *nuclear war.*"

"It was a necessary pre-emptive strike." Peter Sumpter said in German.

Dora asked for that to be translated again.

"I am sorry, what are you talking about?" she asked.

"The nuclear strike on China was a pre-emptive strike to prevent their destruction of Europe. Well, I guess that they must have censored that bit of your history."

"Sorry?!" Ortega tried to process that bit. "Did he just say what I think he said?"

Kinoster nodded and as Sumpter spoke again, he continued to translate.

"Governor Rice said as much in her statement. She had received clear and unambiguous evidence of a plan by the Republic of China to destroy the European Union with the connivance of their traitorous leadership. The New Confederacy sacrificed itself for the survival of European civilisation."

Dora tried to read this man's expression. He either knew that this was complete nonsense and was just pretending to believe it... or genuinely believed it.

"Your leader was completely sick in the head. There was never a China Plan, it existed only in her twisted imagination."

"Are Europeans enslaved?"

"No..."

"You would say that, wouldn't you? You're clearly one of the regime's thugs. You look like a thug."

Ortega asked for that to be translated again. Then, she reached for a plastic beaker and threw it at Sumpter's head. He ducked to one side and the green container clattered against the wall.

"Yes, I'm a thug. I'm giving strong consideration to throwing you out of the airlock right now."

Sumpter raised his eyebrows.

"Well, if you were in my power, I'd do the same. You're clearly some form of race traitor. A Muslim President and you happily serve under him?"

He gestured to a photograph on her wall of a man wearing a suit and a presidential sash. Dora looked at it.

"Yes, that's President Said-Alvarez. He's not only Muslim, but he's also half Mexican and half Sudanese."

"Wow, even worse," Sumpter said.

Dora decided that enough was enough here. This guy was clearly not fit for modern society. Time to give him something that he would not forget for a long while. She got up and removed her face mask.

"Now, I don't know why you didn't blow yourself up with the rest of your gang..." she said, walking towards him.

"Well, I wanted to continue the fight..."

Dora grabbed his lapels. Kinoster paused briefly and then continued to translate; Dora had done this sort of thing on multiple occasions.

"You're not going to be continuing anything. We're going to search through our archives, find something to charge you with - and lock you up - for the rest of your life."

She released him, started to step back... then sneezed into her sleeve.

"You might not live that long. I'm nursing a mild cold and I bet your immune system hasn't encountered our cold virus before."

Chapter 10

The wake for Grant Robinson was a typical Spacee affair; namely one with a fair amount of drinking and a large amount of food consumption.

Maria Penzance was present at the wake, making small talk with some miners who had clearly turned up for the free food. She was dressed in a black dress with black jacket, looking distinctly numb at the whole thing.

The others had kept their distance, wary of what to say. Sunita Kumar watched her out of the corner of her eye as she talked to Rebecca Carrington.

"You remember the time that we asked Grant to get a long weight and a left-handed screwdriver from the hardware store at Plaistow?" she asked.

"Yes," Rebecca said as she took a bite of fig roll with a smile.

"I wasn't expecting him to actually turn up with both items. Turned out I was the subject of the prank." Sunita smiled.

"Yes, that was Lionel Stevens' idea," Rebecca said. "He had that happen with apprentices all the time, so he decided to get his own back."

"Did Grant know?"

"Yes, because I told him. What did you do with the weight?"

"It's in my room as a reminder."

Rebecca looked at the framed photograph of Grant on the table.

"Can we get Grant's life insurance pay-out transferred to Maria?" she asked. "She may not have legally registered the relationship, but in the circumstances..."

"Good idea. She will need the money, especially after she gets out of prison."

"You know I've been in prison."

Sunita's mouth dropped open.

"Shut the front door!" she said rather too loudly. "What for?"

Several others turned to look at her, with Maria walking over.

"Behaviour non-conducive to good public order," Rebecca said.

"What did you do?" Sunita asked.

"I did a sermon in the cathedral having a go at a Bishop for sleeping with a member of the choir."

"So, one of those 'offences' that aren't actually crimes. What did you get?"

"They gave me a month in prison and 50 lashes."

"Lashes?!" Maria asked, suddenly perking up. "Like with a whip?"

"Yes."

"Did you get scars?"

Sunita thought that Rebecca was going to tell Maria off, but she looked down instead.

"Yes. All up my back. I would show you, but this isn't the appropriate place for it."

"I don't want to go to prison," Maria said. "Especially a Terran Union one. They make you do mining, or construction."

"We don't want you to go to prison either," Sunita agreed.

"This has been a horrible month..." Maria said, starting to well up. "I wish we'd never seen that ship..."

"Me too," Sunita said then gave Maria a hug.

****

The Terran Union hospital ship *Julia Herriot* took on eight new patients. They were examined for any infectious illnesses.... and one of them was found to have had a rhinovirus. Specifically, HRhV-2585-LC14. This was something was a *modern* illness that gave most humans a moderate cold. For Peter Sumpter, it required him to have supplemental oxygen and antibody treatment. He could have only gotten the infection on

Margaret Carter and the ship's chief medical officer put that in his report. The report was sent to Marshal Wald, who stuck it in the electronic filing cabinet.

****

Shortly after the wake was concluded, Sunita was in the ship's gym, doing some push-ups to shift the baby fat, with Dr Wilmslow monitoring her heart rate as part of the fortnightly check-up that she did on all the crew.

"How are you feeling, Sunita?" Hannah asked the Third Officer.

"About what?" Sunita replied.

"Grant."

"Trying not to think about it."

"That's not always healthy behaviour. Talk about your feelings."

"He died in front of me. Poisoned by that Nazi witch. One minute he was talking, the next he was... I can't even remember his last words before the cyanide hit him in the face."

"Is this the first time you've seen someone die?"

"No... but it was the first friend's death I've been fully conscious for. I wasn't fully with it for much of the Saratoga trip, when Jack got impaled by that tree.

"I've seen plenty of dead bodies before, but Grant was the youngest person I've seen dead... He had so much ahead of him... and now he's gone."

"How do you feel about Maria shooting Ava Rice?"

"I don't know. I don't generally condone unprovoked murder, but I think that so-called woman is someone you can make an exception for..."

Sunita's comm rang and she moved to pick it up, laying down on the floor as she spoke.

"Hey, Darius," she said. "What is it?"

"We've got some people here from the Helvetios Procurator's Office that want to interview you, under oath. Plus, Maria's lawyer."

"When?"

"Now if you can help it. Feel free to shower first."

"Got it, out."

Sunita got up off the matt.

"Get me my jacket," she instructed Mary.

****

"This is a recorded deposition with Sunita Kamala Anwar Kumar on 22 August 2619, taken at Zug Station in the Helvetios System."

Sunita, still rather sweaty, was sitting in the canteen of *Tulyar* facing four lawyers, a judge, and a gendarme.

She had seen Maria's two lawyers before and had of course encountered Captain Bowler as well. The magistrate was new to her, as was the blue-uniformed procurator now standing in front of her. New and somewhat intimidating.

Alexandra "Call me Sasha" Pilkington had a black glove on her right hand and the not quite 100% natural grip of someone with a recently acquired artificial limb from the way she held her mug. Her right eye had been replaced with a robotic one as well.

As the crew of *Tulyar* were not exactly going to be sticking around for however long it took to bring Maria Penzance for trial, their evidence would be handled by deposition; with prosecution, defence, and Judge Dred Scott asking them questions in turn. The whole thing was being recorded and would be played at the trial.

This process had brought back memories of Sunita's own encounters with the law; both of them. The first case back she was sixteen when she had stolen a shuttle, taken it for a joyride twice around a planet and then crash landed in a lake, causing quite a bit of damage. That had gotten her six months in a secure training centre, later reduced to three months on appeal. The second time, when employed on a cruise ship, she had attacked a passenger for bigoted comments about an alien crew member. That had gotten her a fine and community service. Naturally, she had lost her job as well. In both cases, she had faced some rather unpleasant prosecutors so turning up in her particular not fully smart state was a metaphorical two fingers to the entire profession.

"Are you ready to be sworn in?" Dred Scott asked.

"Yes, let's get on with it." Laura Stewart passed over a copy of the Bhagavad Gita, the holy book of Sunita's Hindu faith. She placed her left hand on it and raised her own.

"I swear by Gita that the evidence I will give shall be the truth, the whole truth and nothing but the truth," Sunita replied, solemnly and firmly, meaning every word. Spacees took their oaths seriously.

"Mrs Kumar," the magistrate began. "Tell me, in your own words, the events as you recall them."

"Which events?" Sunita asked.

"The ones leading up to and including the shooting of Ava Rice."

Sunita, who had not really prepared for all of this, began to recall what had transpired in in the couple of days leading up to the shooting, explaining her experiences and what she saw. Sometimes she went back to correct herself.

"And then I heard the gun shot," Sunita said. "You have the security footage from the brig, so I don't know why you're asking me about this."

"I want to get an idea of the state of mind of Maria Penzance before the shooting."

"I didn't see her at all between my leaving the ship and the shooting."

Sasha Pilkington raised her pen.

"Is Ms Penzance known to be a violent person?"

"No more violent than the average human being, no." Sunita replied.

"Why then would she have a blackjack in her room?"

"I imagine for personal protection. She is a 19-year-old woman and not exactly the strongest physical fighter."

"Did you issue her the weapon in question?"

"No, I did not."

"Are you sure?"

"Absolutely certain. We have extendable batons on *Tulyar*, not saps, blackjacks or coshes."

"Has she ever used physical force on board the ship?"

"Only to perform the Heimlich Manoeuvre."

"Are you aware that she expressed a desire to shoot Ava Rice while on *Tulyar*'s bridge?"

Sunita looked confused...

"When was this?" she asked.

"It was on the bridge voice recordings. During the hostage situation."

"Objection," Johanna Orlov-Park said. "I am not sure that we can have Sunita comment on something that she wasn't present for."

"Sustained," the magistrate said.

"I will rephrase. Did you ever hear Maria Penzance express any animosity towards Ava Rice before the shooting?"

"No, because I didn't talk to her between learning of Rice's existence and the shooting. I'm not surprised that she would feel some animosity towards her. Virtually any decent human would. Any decent sapient would."

"When you saw Penzance in the brig after the shooting, what did she say?" Pilkington asked.

"I wasn't exactly recording it."

"No-one was. You don't have an audio channel on your brig security feed."

"Why would we?"

"I am asking the questions here, Mrs Kumar. What did she say?"

"I believe it may have been along the lines of..."

Sunita said what she recalled hearing Maria say.

"I'm not sure that would have been physically possible," Sasha Pilkington remarked, provoking some slight laughter. She did not seem to find it funny.

The rest of the prosecution questioning was easy. Johanna Orlov-Park then took her turn.

"Are you aware of Maria's relationship with Grant Robinson at the time of his death?" she asked.

"I wouldn't say that I knew for certain," Sunita replied. "But I could tell something was up by their body language.

"Body language?"

"Their usual physical proximity to each other, the way they looked at each other."

The judge spoke up at this point.

"This is calling for speculation and an assessment of body language from a non-expert in the field. It's not exactly admissible... and by the defendant's own statements, she believed she was in a relationship with the deceased. I think we can safely take that as the case in the absence of any compelling evidence to the contrary."

Johanna changed tack.

"Would Maria have known that Grant was dead at the time of the shooting? You were with him."

"I don't honestly know. It isn't something that occurred to me to ask in all of this," Sunita replied, being perfectly honest.

"Did you consider yourself shooting Ava Rice after this?"

Dred Scott raised a hand.

"What is the relevance of that question?"

"Clapham Omnibus Test," Johanna replied.

"I'm not familiar with that one."

"It's a concept from the pre-UEG British law that has been incorporated into Terran case law. It's what an average reasonable sapient person would do in the circumstances."

"And are you suggesting that the average sapient person would shoot Ava Rice?"

"I am saying that they would at least consider this."

Dred Scott looked up, looked down and then took a sip of his water.

"This sounds awfully like a discussion for an appeal court. *Not* a deposition."

The rest of the deposition after that stuck to matters of fact.

****

In the afternoon of the following, Louisa Landry and Sunita Kumar stood watching as their new cannon was installed by a series of automated drones that carefully lowered it into place. The old turret was to be sold for scrap metal.

"I've bought us some Killer Tomatoes," Louisa said.

Sunita looked very confused, wondering why Louisa was buying a strange foodstuff.

"Sorry, killer tomatoes? Why would you buy those?"

"I forgot, you're a gun hamster. I'm the former Terran Union Navy Starman who worked on a gun turret for six years."

"Of course, you did. TNS *Semyon Randall*, I seem to recall."

"Indeed, *David Osanto*-class destroyer. Anyway, Killer Tomatoes are what we called the red-coloured target drones we used to train with. There are also Killer Apples, Killer Oranges... even Killer Plums."

"So, why have we got them?"

"To test the new gun on."

"Right, got it."

"Also, I'm going to be rather glad when we get out of here. Bit concerned about the security of this station. Especially with Ava Rice here."

"You think someone's going to break her out?"

"They may be a *small* minority, but there are still some racists out there. It's more a comment I overheard about this place's defence system."

"Really? What about it?"

"It's faulty. Has been for a week."

****

The following morning's meeting was commenced by Vanessa Widomski.

"I've got several pieces of news," she began. "It's been agreed that Maria Penzance is going to go to Basel pending her trial there, which is provisionally booked in for six weeks' from now. They don't have a huge number of major cases in this system for obvious reasons and everyone wants to get this over and done with."

Sunita nodded.

"Quite right," she observed.

"We've been told by New London to wrap up our business here and go. There are another four depositions to be done today. After that, we will travel to Basel and conduct our interviews with the media for Helvetios Daily. That will take a whole day and is also going to involve a camera crew filming parts of our ship. So, hide anything you don't want on camera."

"Who do they want to talk to?"

"We're limiting it to the key players. Have you ever done a television interview before?" Vanessa asked.

"I did one after I got the Royal Order of Excellence," Sunita replied.

"How did it go?"

"I farted during the interview."

"Mrs Kumar, that is too much information," Vanessa said in a disapproving manner.

"Ma'am."

"Well, you know what it's like then. So, tell us."

"Longer than you might think. They will allow you to do multiple takes of an answer if you've not got it quite right... and they may cut a lot of the footage out. Did they say how long they're looking to make the documentary?"

"Two hours, apparently."

"In TV speak, that's 85 minutes. The rest will be adverts."

"I detest adverts."

Maria was sitting in her room, thinking about the shooting. That was pretty much all she thought about these days. She might be able to do something a few minutes and then it kept coming back. Playing repeatedly in an endless loop.

She had seen a doctor on the station, who had given her some limited antidepressants. The prosecutors did not want her killing herself, but they also did not want her completely remorseless. She had been doing some reading about Terran Union prosecutors. They were one of the few groups of officials in the super state that you probably would not be able to bribe. The judges, the police, the prison officials were often partial to a bit of baksheesh – but the prosecutors, no chance. If anything, they would add bribery to the charges against you for even trying.

She was having mixed feelings about the whole thing. She had shot an unarmed defenceless woman – who was also a genocide-committing war criminal who had just murdered her boyfriend.

The communicator on her desk rang. The caller ID was Laura Stewart's office and she moved to pick up the handset, to make sure that the other half of the call could not be heard by anyone eavesdropping in his room.

"Maria, it's Laura," her lawyer unnecessarily informed her, then continued. "We've got a transfer for you to Basel ahead of your trial. Small apartment in Chamonix Town, a short walk from the court. Place we own for people like you."

"People like me?" Maria asked.

"Those on bail with no permanent accommodation in system. Happens more often than you think, especially with miners who get their vessel seized as evidence or have to use it for the bond money."

"So, when I am going?"

"Tomorrow evening, 1900. Mail ship has a space for us."

"Got it."

"Also, *Tulyar* is departing today. The crew want to say goodbye to you. The court has agreed that provided lawyers present."

"Why lawyers?" Maria asked.

"Make sure you don't intimidate any witnesses."

"Have you seen the crew of *Tulyar*? They're not exactly the kind of people you can intimidate."

****

The parting was done in the conference suite of the hotel. Pilkington and Orlov-Park stood next to the big table, remaining in earshot.

They had come in one at a time, limited to one or two at a time. Maria had engaged in a lot of crying... and now Rebecca Carrington came in with her husband. She was dressed in her Second Officer's uniform, the standard trousers replaced with a long skirt. She wore an artificial flower in her hair and some long earrings.

"Rebecca..." Maria said, lowering her head, unable to look her former colleague in the eyes.

Rebecca Carrington thought for a second, trying to find the right preamble, and then just went for it.

"I forgive you."

Maria looked up.

"You forgive me?" she said softly. "Just like that?"

"Yes," she said after a slight pause. "I forgive you. I assume you are sorry."

"Yes, yes, I am..."

"I might not see you again. I hope to one day. I understand why you did what you did. I think you know deep down that it was wrong, and I think that you know deep down that you will need to take responsibility for your actions."

Maria looked confused.

"Don't you just have to say sorry to God and that's it? You're forgiven."

Rebecca could have made some cutting remark. Instead, she chose to sit down, extended her hands, and took Maria's in them.

"Maria, you should try to do what you can reasonably do to make amends to the person you have wronged."

"They're not going to exactly let me see Ava Rice to apologise to her... and I am not going to apologise to the woman who killed Grant."

"No, I'm not asking you to do that... but it might be a good idea to plead guilty."

"I'm considering a plea bargain. I don't want to go to prison though."

"I know. I will pray that justice is done for you. I know that God has a plan... and he might work in mysterious ways."

* * * *

Once everyone had said their goodbyes, *Tulyar* was cleared to leave. The undocking process at a relatively small station like this was easy; just ask to go and make sure you did not hit anything on the way out.

****

"We've got some more ore to pick up when we get to Basel," Alexander Carrington said as he sat in bed, waiting for his wife to brush her teeth. They were both off shift at the moment and since *Tulyar* could handle a simple undocking without them, getting some sleep was of a higher priority.

"Indeed, honey," Rebecca said as she spat out the remains of the toothpaste and reached for the cup to fill it with mouthwash.

"You ever been on TV before?" Alexander asked.

"Yes, back on Dom Pennsylvania."

"They have TV there - really? I thought they'd find it sinful."

"Well, the stuff is heavily censored – but they find it very useful for broadcasting services and things like that, especially for those who can't physically go to church."

"So, what were you on?"

"I was in a Bible Bee when I was fourteen. It's where school quiz teams have to answer trivia questions about the Bible. Sometimes rather hard ones."

"Any that you remember?"

Rebecca thought for a second.

"Ah yes. Which King of Judah got leprosy after burning incense on the altar of the Temple in Isaiah Chapter 26?" she recited.

"Er... Lot?"

"No, Uzziah," Rebecca replied, filling her cup with mouthwash.

"I'm useless at remembering that sort of thing. Don't ask me to remember Bible quotes."

Rebecca smiled. She swigged the mint flavoured liquid around for her mouth for the requisite 30 seconds, then spat it out.

"I think God wants to us to focus more on loving him and our neighbour than learning the Bible off by heart."

She rinsed the water down the sink and turned to her husband.

"Bathroom's yours."

****

"Foxtrot Papa Five-Five-Zero-One-Five, you are now leaving the station control zone. I would say thank you for visiting, but to be honest, I think we're as glad to see the back of you as you are of us. Zug Station, out."

Vincent Nguyen pressed the red button on his console to terminate the call with *Tulyar*. The whole circus round here was starting to come to an end, with pretty much everyone involved due to head out in the next day, either on their private transports or via the mail ship. Then he could get back to normal, although there would of course be the ceremony for the commendations likely to come the station personnel's way.

He removed his headphones and got up from the console to head to the water cooler. His shift had just an hour to run and then he was going to the weekly pool tournament at Happy Larry's Bar. A 500-credit top prize was particularly appealing, and he had a chance...

He had just put his mug under the spout when the alarm klaxon went off.

Chapter 11

Fifty kilometres from Zug Station, a Pewter GTI-7 mining ship was standing, apparently waiting for a docking port to become available.

This vessel was a 'breaker' designed to tear apart small asteroids into more manageable chunks that a dedicated 'harvester' ship could then pull in for extraction. As such, it carried six lasers, two large cannons... and a 25-kiloton Atomic Separation Munition.

Without any warning, it fired the two cannons at Zug Station, using all six barrels of each of the two revolver type weapons.

Twelve rounds streaked quickly across the short distance, slamming into the fire control and search radars of Zug Station.

The station's heat-seeking missile launcher activated, swinging around under local control to engage the attacker. A single missile started to ignite, its drive powering up to full speed... but instead of coming out of the launch rail, it fired *inside* the turret. The fuel exploded, then cooked off the high explosive warhead.

****

Vincent felt the station start to drift to his right. The station keeping engines that stopped this sort of thing would get going in a second, but that explosion did not sound good.

"Winchester - get a damage report! I'm going to contact this idiot and ask him what he is playing at!"

Vincent moved rapidly back to his console. A quick move of his trackball and he had selected the contact, named *Saffron Walden*, then pressed the button to make a secure radio connection.

"*Saffron Walden*," he said at a normal but very firm voice, "what are you playing at?"

He knew the owner of that ship. Peter Morris. A xenophobe – in the sense that he did not like aliens and had been banned from all the bars on the station after verbally abusing a Gan. But he did not seem the type to conduct a violent attack on the facility.

"Listen up Zug," came the voice of Peter Morris. "I'm here for one reason and one reason only. Ava Rice."

Vincent was glad this was audio only as his mouth dropped open.

"Sorry, Ava Rice?" he said.

"Simple, I want her released to me. Or I destroy the station. You have twenty minutes. I have an Atomic Separation Munition and I am willing to use it."

"That's not in my power to do."

"I know that. Run it up the chain. Any attack on me and I will use the device."

Morris disconnected and called his commander. He explained the situation.

"I can't give him what we don't have." Major Tamm replied.

"Sorry, sir?" Vincent asked, then realised what she meant before she answered.

"We discreetly shipped Ava Rice out ten hours ago."

"I am not sure he'll believe that."

"Make him believe it. We've got serious casualties around the missile launcher section and our fire control radar is wrecked. If we fire on local control, he will fire back before we can kill him. Same with launching our fighters."

****

Vanessa was in her office when Clarissa's voice came out via the ship wide intercom.

"All hands, there's been explosions on Zug Station!"

She put down her coffee and walked quickly through the open door to the bridge. Rebecca Carrington swiftly vacated the Captain's chair and Vanessa took her place.

"Sunita, how far are we away from Zug?" she asked.

"Five hundred kilometres. I'll go back and check the radar plots, see who if anyone fired," Sunita replied.

"I'm betting someone did. Mr Forgan get us back to the station, ready to take on survivors. Mrs Carrington, please get your husband to open the cargo bays so we can take on any lifeboats. Is Ms Landry in the turret?"

"Yes, she is. Well, when you find out who fired at the station, lock them up and get ready to fire when we're in range. Wait for my instructions – or engage should they open fire again."

The ship started to turn, and Vanessa looked to see the damage to the station. There was a large part of the top of it that was now missing...

"Oh yes - go to Red Alert," she added.

****

"We haven't got Ava Rice," Vincent said. "so, you're threatening to kill over a thousand people for one woman who isn't even on the station."

"I don't believe you." Peter Morris was sounding like a villain from a cheap movie. You have eighteen minutes to change your mind and give me what I want."

"I can't do that." Vincent felt damp in multiple places. He hoped it was sweat. He had never been on the receiving end of a hostage situation. Or indeed actually any combat situation. This was common for the Terran Union military, who had not been involved in a major conflict for four decades now.

"Then everyone on that station dies."

Vincent looked at his display. He selected *Tulyar*, which was the only craft currently undocked with a halfway decent weapon. He sent a text message to them.

"Why do you want Ava Rice?"

"Because she needs a statue, not a jail cell."

Vincent put his hand over his eyes. He was one of them as well. A human hater. He knew they existed, but they tended to be very well hidden from society at large. Who would openly say that they believed some humans were less equal than others?

****

Sunita clambered into the new turret with Louisa Landry. She headed over to the radar console, grabbing her own headphones.

"Kumar to Bridge, I'm in the gunner radar seat and turning things on," she said, her hand moving to the plug at the wall to flick the switch.

She then moved to the on switch and the main computer screen started to come to life. She was then greeted with the worst message that any computer user can face in an emergency situation.

She was asked to enter a licence key for her software.

****

"I'm in the turret," Sunita said over the intercom. "That's the good news. The bad news is that I'm having to run through the installation sequence. They wanted a memorable place in case I forgot my password."

"What did you put?" Darius Marri asked.

"Berwick. Place where Daniel and I first played strip poker."

Darius chuckled.

"If we die and the last thought that I have is of you playing strip poker..."

"You'll die happy."

"I wasn't going to say that. We found out what happened from the station. They got fired on by a Pewter GTI-7".

Darius looked at the ship profile on the screen in front of him.

"Six lasers, two 150mm cannon. Could do us some real damage in a fight."

"He'll be carrying an Atomic Separation Munition as well in all likelihood."

"And he wants Ava Rice..."

Sunita swore in Tamil.

"It's a hostage situation then. I think we're fully justified in opening fire in defence of Zug Station."

Vanessa spoke up at this point.

"Have we had a formal request from Zug?" she asked.

"Do we need one?" Sunita asked, sounding rather confused.

"Under the Posse Comitatus Acts, we legally do."

"Well, you get that. Now I'm going to fire when I'm ready, permission slip or not."

Sunita huffed and then signed off.

"If you engage a vessel without it attacking you or someone being attacked by it requests your assistance," Vanessa said, "it is a criminal offence."

"I have heard of cases where pirates have called in for assistance against their own targets," Daniel added.

"Mr O'Hanlon," Vanessa said witheringly, "I really don't think that's relevant here. Send the message, will you?"

****

"You have ten minutes remaining. I also need a live stream to show her being transported, so I know you're not trying to trick me with Jessica the barkeep."

Peter Morris was sounding to Vincent like someone who had watched too many crime movies. Being an effective hostage taker was just as hard as being a pirate; the Airlock Kickers would happily open fire and the hostages could go breathe vacuum. It tended to deter most, but not all, of the terrorists.

"OK, I'll need five minutes to go and get her," Vincent lied. "I will call you back."

Morris disconnected. At that point, a message pinged onto Vincent's terminal. He read the text.

ZUG STATION, THIS IS TULYAR. YOU NEED ANY ASSISTANCE HERE?

Vincent felt a fair amount of relief at this point. There was someone that could assist in the situation here. Equipped with a modern weapon with a gun radar that could tackle a moving target, they were the best option available now that Zug's own weapons were rather ineffective.

They needed a one-hit kill, because if they missed, the next move would be the **ASM** being fired and then they were in a whole world of further pain. The other mining and cargo ships lacked the accurate weaponry to destroy a ship on the first shot.

Technically he needed the request to come from Major Tamm, but he decided that there was no time to wait. He moved to type his reply.

****

The installation sequence was complete. Sunita had skipped at every stage she could and was now the operator of the weapon currently designated 'Mr Fluffy' for no other reason than she needed to put *something*.

"We've got the request," came the voice of Vanessa Widomski. "Fire at will."

"He's not called Will," Sunita said as she selected the target. The radar warmed up, locked onto the target, and fed the data to the main guns.

"Whatever, just kill it!" Vanessa barked.

Louisa Landry called down from her controls.

"Engaging loading sequence now. It'll take about a minute to load all twelve barrels... I want to give him a full salvo to start off with then go to one every five seconds."

Sunita looked at the digital clock on the screen as the seconds counted down. They had to make this shot count or thousands could die.

With twenty seconds left, she heard a loud oath in French, then the ship shook as eight rounds shot out of the barrels in very quick succession.

"What?" she asked.

Louisa swore again.

"Some cargo ship fired first, do I had to join in, it looks like it's going to be a miss from them... nuke powering up..."

Sunita moved over to the porthole and saw their rounds strike home... just as a nuclear warhead came off

Saffron Walden's launch rail. The impact knocked it slightly off course, but it was still speeding towards the station...

"Sunita, turn away!"

She just out of line of sight as the massive flash filled the room...

****

Maria, sitting in her hotel room, had heard the explosions as the first strikes impacted on the station. She did not hear the nuclear bomb go off, but then again, space was silent.

****

Sunita got back up as the flash faded away, moving quickly over to the porthole to see what had happened. A fireball was starting to dissipate from where the device had gone off, just short of the station... and as it cleared, she could see that the reactor section was a wreck. The station itself was now a dark object blocking the stars.

That's the second nuclear detonation I've been next to this year.

Then some lights started to come on for Zug Station.

She then looked at the remains of *Saffron Walden*. It was in multiple pieces and no-one could have survived that. The floating corpse they saw a minute later confirmed her conclusion.

****

Vincent had been out of the line of sight of the explosion, but its impact had been made obvious when the station was plunged into darkness. Then the red emergency lights came on in the control room.

Electromagnetic interference was commonplace in space and a big event like a solar storm was something that stations were built to withstand. The electromagnetic pulse of a close proximity nuclear detonation was something that was also considered in the design of the Laguna-Salyut class of military stations.

So, that wouldn't cause more than a few blown lightbulbs...

"Sound off!" he called to the people in the control tower and got a reassuring number of surnames from the people present.

A quick check determined that there were no injuries bar a banged elbow.

The intercom switched on and he quickly called Major Tamm.

"Control Tower reporting in, only one minor injury."

He noticed that the various departments of the station were also appearing in a conference call. When Engineering came in, they confirmed the main problem.

"The reactor is wrecked," the Chief Engineer reported. "We're down to emergency power and not a lot of it. The carbon dioxide scrubbers have stopped running and they need mains power to run. Without them, the air is going to get pretty much unbreathable in about twenty-four hours. Internal gravity is good for about three hours but will go down over time."

"Three hours sounds like enough time for an orderly evacuation," Tamm added.

"There's another problem. We took a fair bit of radiation from the blast. It varies across the base, but in the areas closest to the blast, we're looking at up to 7 or 8 Grays of personal exposure."

"So, we're looking at Acute Radiation Syndrome and deaths," Tamm said, then swore, "Medical, we're going to have to start triaging people. Get those that can be saved onto a lighter and get it docked to *Tulyar*. Then prepare a sequenced evacuation of the rest."

****

The red emergency lights had come on in Maria's room. She grabbed a torch from her desk and moved over to the barometer that was standard in many rooms on a space station.

Eight hundred millibars. Basically, we're up a small mountain. If it gets much lower too quickly, we'll have a problem.

She opened the door and stepped out into the corridor. Other people were coming out, looking rather confused.

"Everyone, grab oxygen tanks and follow me to the conference room!" Maria ordered. "I think we need to prepare for a sequenced evacuation. Muster point drill."

A sequenced evacuation. The standard method of getting people off a station when it was not in imminent danger of complete destruction. People were assigned priorities in terms of who would leave the station, with the seriously injured, disabled, elderly and children going first. Your evacuation number was something you learned off by heart. As a healthy 19-year-old, Maria was a Category 5 – she was expected to assist in getting the Category 1s out.

She re-entered the room and opened the wardrobe to pull out the emergency oxygen mask and portable tank. It would not be suitable for a spacewalk but was still recommended for any station evacuation in case of an air leak.

The group of six of them arrived in the conference room, where the manager was standing with the guest book. He started to call out the register of guests, who were taking all of this in their stride.

When he called the name of "Darien Fung," he got no response.

"I'll go and get him," Maria said. "Give me a master key."

The manager looked confused.

"You're a guest..." he said.

"I've also got first aid training and am an experienced merchant ship crew member. I'm also a Category 5 person."

"OK," he said, gesturing to the cleaner. "Greta, go with her."

Greta pulled out her master key and the two of them walked quickly down the corridor to Room 19. The cleaner opened the door and stepped inside.

An overweight Chinese man was lying on the bed.

"Mr Fung!" Maria yelled. "Wake up!"

There was no time for niceties here. She stepped over to him and looked at his face. He was breathing, but the left half of his face was sagging.

She remembered the time she had found her grandfather like this. A week later, they had buried him.

"He's had a stroke. Come and help me to grab him."

"We need someone stronger," Greta said. "I'll go and get some help."

****

Tulyar had docked with Zug Station again. Sunita and Dr Wilmslow were talking with the station's Chief Medical Officer via Daniel's console the bridge. Daniel had his hand on Sunita's shoulder to reassure her.

"We can take up to forty people, but there's only space in our medical bay for five stretcher patients," Hannah said. "If we take them to Helvetios, we can get transport sent back over for the rest."

"That will be great. You're the fastest ship with medical facilities here at the moment. We're going to do a bit of triaging to determine who needs to go first," the CMO replied.

"How many people have you got to triage?"

"About forty who were in the worst hit part of the station for radiation and another twenty in the area where the missile launcher exploded."

"Noted."

Hannah's career in medicine had never yet involved triage, that situation where you had many casualties all at once and you had to decide who to treat first... as well as who could not be saved.

"We'll send five reds over each with a medic with them, but can you direct them?"

"Yes, I can do that."

She did not envy Zug Station's Chief Medical Officer in this situation. She herself was going to need a spot of counselling after this. The whole crew would – it was standard protocol after an incident to have a discussion on how they were all feeling.

"I'll go and get the beds ready. Let me know the extent of their injuries."

****

The people in the hotel had managed to find one of the room service trolleys and four of them had loaded the unconscious man onto it. It was not exactly the most dignified thing in the world, but time was of the essence.

Maria, Greta and two others pushed the unconscious Darien Fung down a corridor in the commercial area of the station. Up ahead, they could see a torch light inside what Maria knew was a hardware store. She figured quickly what that person was doing and decided that he really was not a priority at the moment.

It was not like he was exactly going to get out of the station with the gendarmes controlling the exits.

She heard a creaking above her.

"Stop!" she called out. Just ahead of them, a ventilation access panel dropped straight onto the floor with a very loud crash.

"Good thing that you spotted that," Greta said. "Let's get moving."

They followed the signs to the docking area, where four gendarmes blocked an entrance. Several people were all trying to get to their ships, yelling at the military police.

"Get out of the way!" Maria yelled. "We've got a medical casualty here!"

She cried that out three times and the crowd parted. Maria recognised one of the gendarmes who had arrested her and instinctively looked down.

"We'll take it from here," he said. "Now return to your muster point and someone will come get you."

He examined Darien Fung by waving a torch over his face.

"He's had a stroke, I think," Maria says.

"I figured. Eddie, we got a red case here!"

****

Sunita stood in Front Porch again a few minutes later, watching as the first stretcher case entered the docking corridor. Two medical personnel were wheeling the trolley, while a third was holding a drip.

She was with Rebecca Carrington and both were wearing radiation suits. The patients had been merely exposed rather than contaminated by radiation, which reduced their chances of spreading radioactivity around. Neither of them wanted to take any chances though. Sunita had already lost her hair once and had no desire to lose it again.

Hence the Geiger counter that she was holding in her hand.

They would take these people and two evacuation shuttles. The latter would dock in the cargo bay, each carrying walking wounded and the most vulnerable non-injured.

They were then jumping to the inner system where *Julia Herriot* was waiting to take everyone for further treatment, both physical and psychological – the latter would then jump back to Zug station to finish off the evacuation there; *Tulyar*'s part of the assignment would be considered done after that – by the time they got back, the station would have been evacuated.

The patient arrived and the medical technician started to relay the information. Sunita looked down to see a Caucasian man aged forty-five with very red skin with many blisters; he had been working in short sleeves when hit by the radiation. He had taken about four times the amount Sunita had taken on Desolation and he needed medical treatment on the hospital ship if he had a chance to survive. Now he was barely conscious and in clearly in deep pain despite medication.

She waved him over quickly with the counter, found nothing much above background.

"He's clear, go ahead."

There were four more of these to come.

The second had signs of decompression sickness after exposure to near vacuum.

The third was a man who had just had a stroke, found in a hotel room.

It was going to be a long day.

Chapter 12

"So, how many?" Hannah asked as Vanessa Widomski held a printout in her hands, a report sent over from *Julia Herriot.*

Dr Wilmslow was in her medical bay a day later; it had been cleaned thoroughly to remove all medical traces of the incidents that she had dealt with. No-one had died onboard the ship, but the second person they had taken on board had been in a bad way indeed. While the names were on the ship's log, Hannah had consigned them all to the backs of her mind, a necessary professional remove in her opinion.

Think of them as patients, not people, she reminded herself.

"Sixty-two dead," Vanessa said, "with another ten likely. Injuries adding another two hundred to all of that. Maria Penzance not among them, you'll be pleased to know."

Hannah let out a small sigh of relief.

"So, everyone's off the station?"

"It's hooked up to the System Defence Frigate, which is going to bring it closer in for repair works. They think it's repairable." Vanessa sat down on a chair.

"There's a but in there somewhere, isn't there?"

"There seems to have been some serious issues at the station regarding the effectiveness of its defences."

"Well, the missile launcher wasn't exactly supposed to blow itself up, was it?" Hannah remarked sarcastically.

"No. Apparently there were some issues with the emergency bulkheads as well. Parts of the station that shouldn't have depressurised did."

"Which explains the two guys with decompression injuries I got."

"Those were just the red cases. They had a dozen black cases."

Hannah took a sip of her water. Black triage cases were those who were mortally injured and all you could do was ease their pain.

"I wasn't told about those."

"I think they wanted you focussed on your task. They highly praise you in their report. Station Commander has been placed under house arrest pending a full criminal investigation by the Gendarmerie."

"This is turning into a complete cluster isn't it?"

Vanessa nodded.

"There's demands coming from Sol for a full Select Committee to be established in the Terran Union Senate into the 'Ava Rice Affair'."

"I saw the news report. They're wondering why we were hired in the first place to do this. Apparently, we're a bunch of amateurs."

"Well, when we get to Sol, I will have something to say about that. Now, let's take my blood pressure before it rises any further."

****

This was not your everyday tomb.

Located in a special section of the Necropolis of St Sophia's Cathedral in Kyiv, the Tomb of Evhen Baransky may have been replete with the usual frescos and icons of a burial site of a high figure in the Ukrainian culture he had lived him, but the atmosphere was anything but sombre.

As President Said-Alvarez walked with the aid of his cane past the closed ticket office for the Necropolis, flanked by four Dignitary Protection Group guards, the sound of modern pop music could be heard reverberating from the direction of Saint Evhen's last resting place.

The souvenir shop was locked up for the evening, but he could see an array of tacky merchandise on sale, including Baransky Bobble Heads and plushies. To the side, there were colourful displays dedicated to the man's life, including photographs of his many cats.

Said-Alvarez considered going down the stairs, but a twinge in his hip led to his decision he was going to use the lift.

Two guards went with him, while the other two went down the stairs.

As he exited the lift, the two honour guards, dressed in the dark green traditional uniform of Ukraine, complete with patches showing the blue and yellow flag that now served as the banner of the State of Ukraine-Alpha Eridani, came sharply to attention, their ceremonial rifles on their shoulders. This was not their usual stance; they were usually a lot more relaxed.

"At ease," the President instructed. "At full ease."

"Mr President," the female of the two soldiers, with PINDER on her name tag, said as she lowered her weapon. "It's a real honour to meet you. Any chance of a selfie when you have finished here?"

"Of course," he replied, smiling. When you had an approval rating of 76 to 80 percent, depending on the poll in question, you naturally attracted real fans.

He walked past the café, where he purchased two cans of cherry soda from a woman who had stayed behind just to serve him. He handed over the five-credit note and instructed her to keep the change.

He walked down into the centre of the tomb. The sarcophagus itself sat in the centre of a relatively small room that was surrounded on three sides by soft benches. An eternal flame stood just above it, burnt incense wafting towards the vent in the ceiling and making the whole area smell like a cologne advert. The flags of Ukraine, the United Earth Government, the Stellar Confederation and the Terran Union hung at the back, while a simple bunch of yellow flowers rested on top of the sarcophagus, along with a dark blue teddy bear.

On the front of the tomb, in Comic Sans, were the words:

Evhen Ivanovych Baransky
First President of the United Earth Government
Saint and Martyr
16 April 2040 – 17 November 2108

"If you destroy this planet after I have gone, I will not be impressed."

Normally this sort of monstrous lack of taste would be considered sacrilegious, but Baransky had been somewhat of an eccentric and had gotten most of his own way when it came to designing his final resting place. Except for his suggestion about being embalmed and placed in a glass box, although historians thought he was probably joking there.

Said-Alvarez knew this as well. He had written the foreword to the guidebook. Or rather someone had written the foreword for him and he had signed it.

Standing next to the tomb was a pink-skinned man dressed in dark blue uniform. He had white hair like the President and was also carrying a walking stick. His shoulder insignia had four gold stars, indicating his rank of Counsellor-General.

"Moran," Said-Alvarez said, raising his own cane. He had invited the procurator here to brief him on the current legal situation somewhere a bit more discreet than his own Presidential Place in Carthage.

"Mohammed," Moran Anvers, Procurator-General of Terra, replied. Standing on the seats next to him were two glasses. The President handed the cans over to Moran, who filled the glasses with the soda.

"How's Natalie?" the President asked.

"Shaken but not stirred. She's on her way back to Terra with the survivors of *Margaret Carter.* Seems that the captain of the New London Merchant ship has recommended her for a Silver Star."

"There's going to be a bit of a gong show after this. I imagine."

"Considering that she's recommended medals for a number of the other people involved yes, it will. Not to mention all the Purple Hearts we are going to have to give out for the next of kin."

"There's the Senate inquiry of course."

"Suspect that will find fault with a fair few people, but not those who actually boarded the ship."

"Indeed. I'm going to need to make a written submission making clear that I knew *nothing* of all of this."

"Well, Mr President, I know you didn't have a clue about this. I wouldn't have voted for you if I thought you were that sort of politician."

"Thank you, Moran."

Moran raised his glass to the ceiling.

"What are you doing?" Said-Alvarez asked.

"Raising a glass to President Baransky. He frankly deserves it."

Said-Alvarez felt a bit reluctant for a second, then he relented, raising his own glass.

"Well, Evhen. We found her. Over five hundred years later, but we found her. I can't imagine what you went through after deciding to cover this up."

"Thank you, Mr President, for allowing me the trial of my life."

"To Evhen Baransky."

"To Evhen Baransky."

They took a swig.

"Well, we are going to have to rewrite the guidebook to this place. What was that you were saying about the trial of your life?"

"I'm planning to lead the prosecution team personally if Rice is ever deemed fit to stand trial. Another old Jew putting a Nazi where they belong. My second war crimes trial as well."

Said-Alvarez had known Moran Anvers for forty years since they were in the same Rotary Club chapter together, but this was not something that he immediately recalled. He took another mouthful of soda.

"Your second?!" he asked.

"I was a junior prosecutor in the trial of Honey Shredder."

Said-Alvarez tried to recall this.

"The Gan war criminal? Back in 2573?"

"Well, less a junior prosecutor and more a general errand boy. I was twenty-three back then, fresh out of Harvard Law and working under Sayin Thura. I am sure you remember him."

"Attorney General and later ran for President. Lost to Mary Granger."

"Pity considering how Granger turned out. I'm still in touch with his daughter."

"What would you be looking to charge Rice with?"

"The Helvetios chief counsellor, goes by the name of Sasha Pilkington, is getting first dibs over the attack on *Margaret Carter*," Moran explained. "That will be enough for a life sentence. Then we plan to throw genocide, unlawful aggression and unlawful use of weapons of mass destruction at her."

"Weren't there other people on the ship? Can't we charge them over anything?"

"Unfortunately," Moran said. "we don't plan to charge the rest of the survivors with anything."

Said-Alvarez looked confused.

"Not even the hijacking of *Rosa Parks*? The attack on the Starport in Texas? The attack on *Margaret Carter*?"

Moran shook his head.

"No evidence tying them specifically to the Texas attack... certainly not any forensic evidence. It appears that the lockup containing all that burnt down in 2103."

Said-Alvarez sighed.

"Arson to cover their tracks, perhaps?" he mused.

"An arson, yes, but for destruction of other evidence in the trial of someone selling fake antibiotics."

"How ironic. And the other stuff?" he asked, taking a mouthful of drink.

"Since the people who fired the shots at *Margaret Carter* were shot themselves and *Rosa Parks'* own destruction compromised the forensic evidence *there* on the shootings of the crew of *Lambda Sierra*, we'd have to go for a general conspiracy charge and Pilkington is doubtful that she could make it stick due to that fact that you need to prove crew knowledge. Thinks it would be 60/40 on conviction," Moran reported, his tone making it clear he agreed with Pilkington's assessment.

"So, what are we going to do about them?"

"Sasha Pilkington wants to give them an immunity deal."

"Give them an immunity deal?"

"They go into Witness Protection, get new identities and agree *not* go to the press in return for not being charged."

"That sounds sensible, but disappointing," the President said, taking some more drink.

"Then the only thing left is the trial of the woman who shot Ava Rice. I..."

"I am not going to make any public comment on that," Said-Alvarez interrupted. "It is a matter for the Helvetios Superior Court to determine whether Maria P. is guilty or innocent of the charges against her. However, as President I have the right to exercise clemency or pardon if a case if passed up to me by the Clemency Board."

"Duly noted, Mr President," Moran replied with a smile. Said-Alvarez figured that he had got the message. Moran played backgammon with the Chairperson of the Clemency Board and would make sure things were not unduly held up there.

Mind you, it would probably take about a year to reach the Board even then.

****

Because living your life in corridors had been found to be damaging to your mental health, many underground settlements had dug out to create large caverns, about thirty metres tall and the width of your average city block. This allowed the creation of regular buildings inside the caverns, complete with roofs. Big artificial sunlight projectors - often relaying filtered light from the surface when planetary rotation allowed for it – provided a real sense of night and day for residents. The effect looked like a movie set to anyone who had grown up in the real outdoors, but it least it did not rain without warning.

Unless the climate control staff wanted it to.

Vanessa Widomski had been in many of these places over the course of over 20 years as a professional starship crew member and had found them to be very much identical in some regards, but not always the case – sometimes people would customise their habitats to remind them of 'home' – which was mainly the place that the original colonists had hailed from.

As she rode through the streets in a laid-in limousine with the others going for their interview at the studios of Helvetios Independent Television ("HIT shows for everyone!"), she was pleased to note that there had been some local flavour added here. The buildings looked like vintage farmhouses from parts of Terra, with stone lower halves and wood-effect upper halves topped off with a peaked roof; actual wood for buildings was a rarity outside of Garden Worlds due to the fire risks involved.

She was dressed in full uniform without any make-up; she would let the professionals take care of things while they were there. Sunita, with her husband and daughter along for the ride, looked like she was going for a date night that would end in the bedroom. For one thing, she was wearing a *dress*, something which was a rarity for her.

She had some notes about what she was going to say in the interview ahead of her; certain key aspects had to be mentioned. Especially around Maria Penzance.

****

The studio for the interview was the one used for *Helvetios Daily*, HIT's main news programme. A digital backdrop showed the surface of Basel containing an illusion that they were above ground and there was an overall red colour palette to the studio.

Vanessa Widomski sat in a straight red faux-leather chair, with a glass of water by her side, as the camera crew adjusted light levels and the eyeline of the camera to make her look her best. As someone who had done a spot of modelling in her youth, Vanessa had experience in looking good... and waiting around for someone to sort out a fiddly technical bit.

The man interviewing her was called Kyle Minnow, who Sunita had greeted with the obvious pun, "Do colleagues often find you a bit fishy?" when she was introduced to him. He was an urbane man in his forties and from the way he was smiling at Vanessa in particular, he clearly wanted to spend some alone time with her. Vanessa would say a very firm no if he made it explicit and that was enough for nearly all men.

The make-up gentleman leaned in to touch up a bit of her foundation and move a stray hair back.

"Now, Vanessa?" he began. "Can I call you Vanessa?" Minnow asked.

"You can call me by my title. Captain Widomski," she replied.

"Are you good to go, Captain Widomski?" he asked.

"Ready whenever you are."

"We'll do a few minutes of discussion to make sure the sound levels are correct and then start recording. We'll only stop if you ask, we seriously trip on something or it looks like you're too emotional to continue. You can be a bit emotional if you want. The audience will love that."

"Duly noted," Vanessa replied, deciding that she was not going to blub on camera. While humanity in general was much more open about sharing their feelings than some people had in the past, most preferred to keep this sort of thing to a selected confidant or the ship's doctor. It was the latter in Vanessa's case.

****

"So, how did you feel when you were selected to make first contact with *Rosa Parks*?" Minnow asked.

"Well, initially slightly confused. It came very much as a surprise, but after that, I realised what an opportunity it would be," Vanessa replied.

"Financially?"

"It would be remiss to say that it did not cross my mind."

****

"When you saw the ship," Minnow asked. "What was your first impression?"

"That it looked in surprisingly good shape for a vessel that is over 500 years old," Vanessa answered.

"Were you thinking yourself of going on board? Leading from the front?" Minnow followed up.

"No, that did not occur to me. I am a strong delegator and I felt that Sunita Kumar would be the best for the job."

"Why?"

"She has a certain 'street smart' about her, to coin a phrase," Vanessa replied, realising that she sounded like a politician she knew from her private member's club.

"Which you don't have?"

"Not as much as her. Anyway, in a game of chess, you use the pieces in their required roles... No, that's a bad metaphor. Can we do that again please?"

They paused for a minute as Vanessa thought over her answer, then they resumed.

"Sunita had done the research on the vessel; she knew as much as could be reasonably expected in the circumstances. She was also the better trained in zero-G environments."

Vanessa did not mention that she herself was prone to throwing up in them.

****

"When you discovered that Ava Rice was on *Rosa Parks*, what was your reaction?" Minnow changed the topic.

"Initial confusion, shock and then a deep concern for my crew. Along with the crew from *Emilia Plater*. I informed their commanding officer of the situation himself," Vanessa responded, remaining calm and matter of fact.

"Do you believe that the boarding of the vessel should have been held off on until the records on Terra were fully checked?"

"In hindsight, yes. But that is always 20-20."

"Do you think that the President of the Terran Union knew about her presence on his vessel or not? Surely the most powerful human in history would have been told that information?"

"That's beyond my knowledge. He said he had no idea. Whether you believe him or not is another matter."

****

"What are your feelings about your fellow crew member Maria P. who is now awaiting trial for the attempted murder of Ava Rice?" Minnow asked.

"I cannot condone what she did." Vanessa was coming to appreciate this man's interviewing technique, if not necessary his choice of cologne.

"You fired her, did you not?"

"That is correct."

"Do you think she should go to prison for what she did? Surely she was doing the galaxy a favour?"

"I believe that she should face some consequences for her action," Vanessa said, then picking her next words carefully, "but I also believe that the matter should be reviewed by the Clemency Board."

"For a presidential pardon?" Minnow asked, clearly seeking clarification.

"I personally would have never prosecuted her. Does it serve the interests of justice to jail a young woman whose boyfriend was murdered by cyanide spray hidden in a boot? By a woman like Ava Rice?"

Vanessa saw Minnow's smile. The cat had just gotten the cream, and this would be the clip of the interview.

****

After the interview was done, Vanessa watched the others from the control room, noting their general style.

Rebecca Carrington was eloquent, personable, and relatively open about her feelings. She also engaged in some not entirely subtle evangelism, but Vanessa could not fault her for that.

Joaquin was very much focussed on the technical side of things, demonstrating an excellent recall of technical details that would probably end up on the cutting room floor for being too specialist for a general audience.

Hannah Wilmslow spoke honestly about the ethics of trying to save the life of a mass murderer and what she had managed to observe during her time on the ship. She looked forward to reading any medical reports on the surviving icicles. Vanessa was curious as well.

Otto did not have a great deal to say except for the intricacies of docking with an incredibly old vessel. He had never been the most talkative of people and Vanessa predicted he would be nearly entirely cut from the transmitted programme.

Sunita's interview was one for the ages. The woman had a rather filthy charm once you got to know her; she occasionally lapsed into bad language and then apologised straight away. She told some corny jokes and made clear that while she was not a hero, if they wanted to give her a medal, she would accept it. When the interview went out in a week's time, she would likely be the star attraction.

****

Maria, Johanna, and Laura had gone in the service entrance of the Helvetios Superior Court to avoid someone getting a photograph. The building itself was in neoclassical-modern style; it looked like an old building but with all the modern conveniences, like an elevator concealed within a large stone column.

A security guard was waiting for them and they were taken to a conference room where Sasha Pilkington was sitting, flanked by two other prosecutors. All three were dressed in uniform with digital folders in front of them; they were essentially electronic document readers in fancy covers – Procurator blue in this case. *Tulyar* had a few of them for things like customs documents.

"Is this an attempt to be intimidating?" Maria said.

"If you want to take it that way, then we are not going to be having a pleasant meeting," Sasha Pilkington began. "This is Jacob Leander and Louis Danville, who will be my assistants on this case. Please take a seat."

"I'll stand, thanks," Maria said feeling that two could play at the power move game.

"We're here to discuss a plea bargain as we explained over the telephone."

"Well, let's hear your starting offer," Johanna said, lounging back on her chair.

Sasha opened the folder, and the glow of a document was visible inside. However, a privacy screen prevented Maria from seeing what it said.

"We are proposing a seven-year sentence at a low security facility," the Chief Procurator began.

"Do you think that's an appropriate sentence in the circumstances?" Johanna said. "I was thinking of three years' probation and no prison time."

"Your client took a deadly weapon, assaulted a fellow crew member and took her pistol... then shot a defenceless prisoner in the head," Sasha Pilkington replied.

Maria felt something bubbling up inside her. Rage, guilt, grief... she did not know exactly what it was...

"The defenceless prisoner had just killed my client's boyfriend. I think that's an important circumstance that you haven't considered."

"I have considered it. Just because someone murdered her boyfriend it doesn't mean that your client gets to go vigilante."

At that point, Maria grabbed the water jug from the table. It was quite heavy, and she considered her target for a second as the others rose in horror... then threw it against the wall. It bounced off and landed on the floor, ice, water, and lemon spilling out...

"What the..." Sasha began.

"I am not a vigilante! I was acting to avenge Grant, who you can't even be bothered to name! Along with all the other victims of Ava Rice who may never be named as the records of them were destroyed with their cities!

"This whole legal process is a joke because you can't prosecute the real killer, so you decide to take it on the one person who actually *did something*. Well, go choke on a cashew, because I'm done with this plea bargaining – I'll take my chances in court!"

With that, Maria swept a couple of glasses off the table and dramatically stomped out. As the door started to close behind her, she heard a male voice...

"Teenagers, eh? I have two."

She then yelled an obscenity back into the room and headed back for the car.

****

Being an ice queen was not something that you could do all the time. Sometimes Vanessa Widomski just had to let rip the many supressed emotions that she bottled up; something her psychiatrist had suggested during her time in the Margaret Johnson Clinic. Take yourself off somewhere private and just let it all out.

Vanessa returned to the hotel after her interview and rang the hotel asking for a bottle of vodka. One was duly sent up.

"If you hear some loud screaming in the next few hours," she told the delivery guy, "I am not being murdered."

She then set the audio system in the room to blare out heavy metal at the maximum volume. In the absence of the padded cell that she had at home on New London, this was the best she could do.

The pain of the past couple of weeks came out over the next two hours. The exciting opportunity that had turned into so much peril, with the loss of crew members and many deaths resulting. The fact that she was never going to be able to be a truly private person again, being known for the rest of her days as the woman who captured Ava Rice.

Then she went to sleep off the vodka.

****

Maria was back in the apartment that evening. The journey back had passed in silence; both of her lawyers had clearly been afraid of any further reaction from her.

The residence itself was the upper level of a three-storey faux-wood and stone house, with a large array of rugs, a digital effect fireplace and a fridge with a variety of interesting cheeses. Maria was not going to try Stinking Bishop again in a hurry though.

As she ate her pasta, she received a message from Laura.

Hi Maria,

That wasn't actually the worst antics I've seen at a plea bargain session. At least you didn't actually assault anyone. The carpet will dry.

But I think you can safely say any hope of a plea bargain is dead now. Your temper is a real problem here and Johanna is not inclined to call you as a witness in case you insult the judges.

You may not come out well in a trial at all, so our best hope now is to plead guilty and throw yourself at the mercy of the court. They may be inclined to give you a shorter sentence provided you show some seemingly genuine contrition. The facts and the law are very much against you; I would be failing in my duty if I did not advise you of this.

I also must advise you about conditions in Terran Union prisons, as you are not a local. The popular dramas exaggerate, but not by much. I enclose a memoir by Simone Corner, who spent ten years in a *medium*-security facility. I strongly advise you to read it as it will influence your thinking.

Kind regards,

Laura

Maria started to read the attached book over the next few hours. Some of the stuff that went on there was horrific, with gangs ruling the wings and those who did not toe their line likely to suffer horrific injuries on a work duty.

She closed her eyes and thought over the whole thing. Did she really want to spend ten years inside because she believed she had done the right thing?

Had she done the right thing in the first place?

Chapter 13

The case had been scheduled to last for three days. One each for the prosecution and the defence, the third for the judgment. Ten journalists would be allowed into the court to take notes and do sketches, but no broadcast of proceedings would be allowed.

Maria was picked up by a police car with blacked out windows, which then drove to the court. As she approached, she could see a large crowd of people standing outside the courtroom. Many of them were holding signs saying "Free Maria P." or words to that effect, staying in a fenced off area. She could hear two of them even declaring some form of love for her.

The police kept the crowds away from the vehicle and they turned into the downwards ramp that would take them into the 'underground' car park.

They arrived at the entrance to the court for prisoners. One of the guards opened the rear door and let Maria out.

The three of them were taken up a flight of stairs to the cell block.

"You'll need to stay here until you're called," the guard said as he opened the door to a small cell with a table and chair. "I'll leave the door open in case you need the head, but don't leave the floor. Or I'll have to shoot you with my Taser."

Maria got the impression that the guard was only half-joking; he would shoot her if she tried to escape.

"Thanks."

"To be honest, I hope they let you off. I think you did the right thing."

Not that she was planning to escape. The last few days and nights had arguably solidified her desire to get it over with. She was having dreams of Grant... and of Ava Rice... some even of Ava and Grant together romantically. The two of them were interlinked in her mind now and would forever be.

She was dressed in a smart black suit, which had been bought for her court date – something that would be obvious to anyone who looked.

Sitting down, she prayed that justice would be done to her today. The tension continued to build in her mind as she waited for someone to come over and take her upstairs. She was about to go into battle for her very life.

"Miss Penzance," an usher said, "Please come with me."

She got up and followed him. She wondered if this was how people acted when they went to their executions.

He led her up to another set of stairs. She walked up them and found herself in the dock. She had seen these wooden boxes in dramas and documentaries. They had retractable glass shields that could be raised or lowered depending on the security risk from, and to, the prisoner.

The court was pretty much full. An array of journalists and other members of the public sat in the gallery, eagerly murmuring; the spectator area was full up. Ahead of her she saw her lawyers and then the five judges. They were dressed in their black judicial robes, all looking distinguished and slightly frightening. At least they were not wearing wigs like on New London.

"Bailiff, will you please read the charges? Prisoner, please stand." the lead judge said.

The bailiff began to do so, reciting the charge that Maria Penzance had seen dozens of times before now. She closed her eyes, completely afloat from the whole scene. Then she said the single word.

"Guilty."

The court broke into commotion and there was a rapid series of bangs from the gavel.

"Maria Penzance, I had not actually asked you to formally plead," the lead judge said. "Is that to be taken as a formal plea to the charge against you?"

The tension was broken, and she smiled. Time to go into action.

"Yes, I am pleading guilty," she confirmed.

"You understand what you're doing here – that you are waiving your right to a trial and appeal?"

"Yes, Judge Han, I'm guilty," Maria said. "I shot Ava Rice and wanted to kill her. So, I'm guilty. I throw myself on the mercy of the court to do as it sees fit."

"Then it is so recorded. We will now take statements from the prosecution, defence and then yourself to assist us in deciding your sentence."

****

The three-day trial would be done in four hours. The prosecution and defence agreed on pretty much every element of the offence. Maria Penzance herself then explained her own actions.

"I shot Ava Rice out of pure revenge for the murder of the man that I loved. It was a relatively spur of the moment decision based on the knowledge that Grant was dying and then actually dead. I am not sure I can apologise to Ava Rice directly for shooting her, but I know that it was wrong. It robbed you of a chance to send her down for life for the murders she committed. So, I am sorry.

"This is my first offence, so I'd like not to spend too long in prison, but I entrust my face to your mercy."

She sat down and Johanna Orlov-Park gave her a thumbs-up, then leaned over.

"It's going to be OK."

Maria was taken back to the cell to await her sentence. She was now at peace; confession having been good for her soul here. She was thinking about what she would do when she got to prison. How she would try to fit in and survive... if possible, thrive.

After an hour, she was called back again for her sentencing. The lead judge read the summary of the case and the facts they had considered.

"It is abundantly clear that this was a planned act of attempted murder, done with homicidal intent, but after extreme provocation in the most heinous way possible. The Terran Union does not like vigilantes, bounty hunters or others who take the law into their own hands. We take cases like this very seriously. We are also aware that this is your first offence and that a repeat of this matter is very unlikely. You have received abundant good character statements from your former crewmates and that is to your credit.

"We have considered what would be the most appropriate sentence in the circumstances and while there has been some disagreement, we have reached a consensus. Maria Alison Landry Penzance, please stand."

She did so, sensing the anticipation of those present around her. She was ready for whatever they would throw at her.

"This court sentences you to four years in prison..."

She did not have time to process that before the next bit came.

"Suspended for four years. You will also complete the maximum community service sentence of three hundred hours, to be completed when you return to New London.

"You are free to go. Court adjourned."

The hammer fell and the court went wild. Maria sunk down onto the chair, looking up and thanking God for the result. She was free. Out of a job, but free.

****

After standing with her lawyers at the impromptu press conference held on the steps of the courthouse, Maria Penzance was taken back to the apartment she had been staying in. Johanna Orlov-Park watched her now ex-client as Laura Stewart explained the next steps in the process.

"The court will issue you a travel warrant that can be exchanged for passage back to New London," Laura explained. "As you were convicted, you would normally have to pay for this, but a little bird told me that an anonymous donor will do that for you."

Natalie Anvers, Johanna thought, *I will add it to her bill, and she'll accept it without question. Along with the other miscellaneous charges.*

Laura continued, demonstrating to Johanna a strong knowledge of practical details that would help her in her future career. Sometimes lawyers got a bit too theory based and lost sight of the fact that people's lives were at stake.

"We'll contact Gemma Cook Travel and get things booked. We're off the main liner routes, but we should be available to find a service that gets you to a major hub. Possibly CISC or Hyades Line."

"What about the community service?" Maria asked.

"A message will be sent via the nearest New London Consulate. Not sure where that is."

"Biham. I looked it up."

"They will make the arrangements for you on your return. I suspect they'll give you something appropriate to your skills; your case likely attracted some public sympathy over there."

"When can I get out of here? I want to see the stars again."

"Next day or two. I assume you don't want to see any more press?"

"No, thank you!"

Johanna asked to use the bathroom. Once inside, she opened her personal communicator and found the banking app, authorising the second half of the payments she had made to the private accounts of three Superior Court Judges.

****

As *Tulyar* was approaching the exit point of its journey through hyperspace to the Teegarden system, Vanessa Widomski was sitting in her office reviewing some market intelligence when her intercom rang.

"Widomski here. What is it, Daniel?" she said.

"I've just received a beacon message from New London. Addressed to you," the communications officer said.

"Send it through."

She started the decryption process and five minutes later to read a fairly long message.

VANESSA, MY HEARTIEST CONGRATULATIONS ON THE WAY THAT YOU HANDLED THE SITUATION WITH GS ROSA PARKS. WE HAVE JUST RECEIVED THE FULL NEWS REPORTS ON NEW LONDON.

With the distances from Helvetios to New London, it could take six weeks for anything non-Beacon to traverse the distance if it went via the fast mail ships. Longer if it did not.

THE CR 20 MILLION FINDERS FEE HAS BEEN TRANSFERRED INTO OUR ACCOUNTS AND WILL BE DISTRIBUTED IN THE

STANDARD RATIO TO YOUR PERSONAL ACCOUNTS.

500,000 credits. Not to be sniffed at. Vanessa tried to do the currency conversion into New London pounds in her head, then decided to read on instead.

NO REWARD FOR FINDING AVA RICE. SHE WAS DECLARED DEAD AFTER ALL.

Pity. Some more cash would have been nice. Still, I can pay for my extension.

MARIA PENZANCE HAS RECEIVED FOUR YEARS, SUSPENDED, ALONG WITH 300 HOURS OF COMMUNITY SERVICE. DON'T KNOW HOW THAT HAPPENED. SUSPECT BRIBERY WAS INVOLVED. NOT COMPLAINING HERE. CPS HAVE TOLD ME THAT THEY WOULD NOT HAVE FILED CHARGES – NOT IN PUBLIC INTEREST. IT HAS ALSO BEEN AGREED SHE WILL DO COMMUNITY SERVICE HERE.

I HAVE MADE THE EXECUTIVE DECISION TO CONVERT HER GROSS MISCONDUCT DISCHARGE TO ADMINISTRATIVE SEPARATION. THIS WILL CLEAR HER FOR FUTURE EMPLOYMENT WITH ANOTHER COMPANY. SHE IS ALSO BOOKED ECONOMY CLASS TRANSIT VIA PEGASUS LINES AND HYADES LINES TO ARRIVE ON 14 JANUARY NEXT.

Vanessa took a sip of her glass of water.

HAVE BEEN INFORMED BY PRIME MINISTER THAT HE WISHES TO AWARD SUNITA KUMAR ROYAL CROSS AND REBECCA CARRINGTON DISTINGUISHED SERVICE MEDAL AS PER YOUR RECOMMENDATION. TERRAN UNION ARE CONSIDERING MEDALS AS WELL, PRECISE ONES TO BE CONFIRMED.

Vanessa took a second sip, then almost spat out her water at the next bit.

PRIME MINISTER HAS ALSO ACCEPTED MY RECOMMENDATION TO APPOINT YOU COMMANDER OF THE ORDER OF ST MELLITUS.

Oh, wow. She had thought she would get the CSM gong at some point, but it was generally a retirement present. It was one rank below a knighthood!

YOU WILL OFFICIALLY KNOWN AS CAPTAIN THE HONOURABLE VANESSA GARBO WIDOMSKI, CSM MST(OFF) NP. THE NEW BUSINESS CARDS ARE ON US.

LOOK FORWARD TO SEEING YOU BACK ON NEW LONDON FOR TEA AND MEDALS. THE DARJEELING CROP IS LOOKING GOOD THIS YEAR.

HAPPY FLYING

MERCHANT ADMIRAL SIR ELEANOR CORTEZ KSM MST(NEWLON)

PS THERE'S A NEW TARANTULA WAITING
FOR YOU WHEN YOU GET HOME. HE'S
CALLED GEORGE.

"Well, Miss O'Hanlon" she said to Kimberley, who
was sitting in a carrier next to the window sucking on her
dummy, "shall we go and tell your mother what she's
won?"

****

Milos Tran, Acting Director of the Helvetios Deep
Space Monitoring Network, sat in the office that his
predecessor had been in a month earlier before going
on 'gardening leave' at the request of the Defence
Commissioner. While Shepherd had followed the letter
of the procedure correctly, including hiring civilians to
make initial contact, Vice Admiral Lenka Rybar had felt
that he had acted too quickly and that the fact *Rosa
Parks* was not on the colony ship database should have
raised more red flags than it did.

And there had been red flags; ones with swastikas
on. As he ate his vat-grown chicken sandwich while re-
reading over his submission to the Senate Select
Committee on the Ava Rice Affair, his mind turned to
the woman who had been the cause of all this trouble.

She was now lying in a coma somewhere on
Helvetios, her location a closely guarded secret. At
some point, she would likely wake up and an evaluation

would have to be made on whether she could stand trial. Whatever happened, she was now in a world far different from what she had wanted when she had committed her act of genocide.

So much for the dreams of Ava Rice, he thought, then saw that a new message had come in about a comet being discovered heading towards Helvetios.

An ancient proverb came to his mind about everyone being famous for about fifteen minutes. His fame was over... but for the crew of *Tulyar*, it was likely just beginning.

Epilogue

In an isolated room in the upper-class section of Basel City, a month later, Ava Rice lay in a hospital bed, hooked up to a string of monitors. Her hair was showing extensive black roots after three months in a coma.

Oscar Kansas was a rich mine owner who had offered to take on the care and custody of the unconscious Ava Rice. He had agreed to provide a million-credit bond for keeping her safe and secure; there was no prison in the Union willing to have Rice in its medical bay indefinitely and Basel General could not lock down an entire ward for possibly years on end.

Kansas was to all appearances a pillar of the community. He had hired a highly competent nursing team to look after his charge in a dedicated private wing of his mansion.

He had chosen not mentioned that he was a collector of Nazi memorabilia, including possessing Hermann Göring's Field Marshal baton, stolen from a museum on Terra.

He was now sitting at the side of her bed, admiring the biggest trophy in his collection. Whose eyes were starting to flick open...

Now to see if her language skills have survived the bullet, he thought.

"Eh, eh..." Ava said.

"Good evening, Leader Rice." Kansas said in German. "Welcome to Basel."

"You speak German?"

Rice looked down at her legs.

Probably lost muscle coordination. She might take months to get that back.

"Yes, I do. Some of us still admire you. You showed a willingness to act when others just talked. You saved Terra."

"No, I didn't. It's got a Muslim as President..."

"The nuclear war was what we needed to deal with the excess population on the planet. Unfortunately, you're going to have to be handed over to the authorities for that to face trial where the lead prosecutor is likely to be a Jew."

"I planned for a trial... then I... what happened?"

"You were shot by a gypsy. Clearly to keep you from grandstanding like that. Who is to say they won't let you die in prison?"

"So, what now? What for the white... race?"

"Gone, basically. So much of our blood has been diluted. There are so few people willing to fight for that now. The war is lost. We have been replaced by a single World Government."

Ava looked crestfallen.

"Then it's over."

"There is a new fight now. Our very human species is under threat. From goblins, koalas and other animals."

"Goblins?"

"Aliens. We met actual aliens. They are starting to live among us. Taking our jobs, our land. Infiltrating our defences. Preparing for the day they hope to bring us down."

Ava looked plaintively at him.

"But, dear Ava, before you go to prison, you should know that some of us are working to defend humanity. We are called the Human Defence League."

"Can't you get me out?" she asked.

"Not in your current condition. We did try to rescue you from Zug Station, but our agent messed up the operation. Now it will be a lot harder. But we are going to try." Kansas said.

"That's good to know. I will await your rescue."

Key Characters

Helvetios

- Natalie Anvers, Science Officer, TUSS *Emilia Plater*
- Henry Bowler, Procurator, Zug Station
- George Dirk, Commanding Officer, TUSS *Emilia Plater*
- Vincent Nguyen, Terran Union Navy Control Corps
- Johanna Orlov-Park, Partner, Truman & Coolidge Partnership
- Dora Ortega, Commanding Officer, TUMCS *Margaret Carter*
- Sasha Pilkington, Chief Procurator, Helvetios System
- Ava Rice, Former Province Leader of Dakota, New Confederacy
- James Shepherd, Director, Helvetios Deep Space Monitoring Network
- Laura Stewart, Advocate, Truman & Coolidge Partnership
- Peter Sumpter, Former Officer, New Confederacy Protection Detachment
- Katrin Tamm, Commanding Officer, Zug Station

- Milos Tran, Shift Leader, Helvetios Deep Space Monitoring Network

Sol

- Evhen Baransky, Former President of the United Earth Government
- Max Govan, Branch Manager, Lagos Branch of Swiss Bank
- Albert Mbeki, Chief of Staff, Terran Union Colonial Office
- Jacob Radlett, Secretary of State, Terran Union Colonial Office
- Mohammed Said-Alvarez, President of the Terran Union

Fast Transport Ship *Tulyar*

- Alexander Carrington, Cargo Chief
- Rebecca Carrington, Navigator and Second Officer
- David Forgan, Chief Pilot
- Sunita Kumar, Security & Safety Officer and Third Officer
- Louisa Landry, Fire Officer
- Joaquin Lugar, Deputy Engineer

- Darius Marri, First Officer
- Clarissa Müller, Chief Engineer
- Daniel O'Hanlon, Communications Officer
- Kimberley O'Hanlon, a baby
- Maria Penzance, Shuttle Pilot
- Lyta Qarpik, Boatswain
- Grant Robinson, Deck Cadet
- Vanessa Widomski, Captain
- Hannah Wilmslow, Ship's Doctor

About the Author

Adam Carpenter was born in the 1980s, but was too busy being a toddler to properly appreciate the culture at the time.

He's been a fan of Doctor Who since before it was cool and, with a strong knowledge of trivia, is generally very handy to have on your quiz team.

Having had an interest in creative writing since primary school, he published his first short novel, 'Murder Planet', in 2020.

More from Adam Carpenter- Collect them all!

- Murder Planet
  978-91-986710-3-2

More from Breaking Rules Europe

- Face of Fear by C. Marry Hultman
  978-91-986710-0-1
- Dawson Junior G3 by Brian Wagstaff
  978-91-986710-4-9
- New Life Cottage by Esther Jacoby
  978-91-986710-5-6
- Liebe ist Warten by Esther Jacoby
  978-91-986710-7-0
- Musing on Death & Dying by Esther Jacoby
  978-91-986710-6-3
- Earth Door by Cye Thomas
  978-91-986710-2-5
- Graffiti Stories by Nick Gerrard
  978-91-986710-1-8
- Punk Novelette by Nick Gerrard
  978-91-986710-8-7

- o Lost Lore and Legends – anthology
    - o Paperback: 9789198671094
    - o Hardcover: 9789198684100

Find us at: www.breakingrulespublishingeuro.com